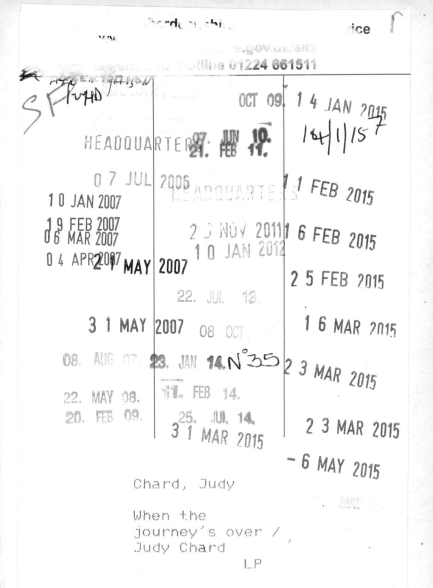

Chard, Judy

When the
journey's over /
Judy Chard
          LP

P   1494211

D0773918

WHEN THE JOURNEY'S OVER

Doctor Helen Elliot has gone to South America to persuade her father, Doctor Steven Elliot, to return to England with her. Helen meets Keith Denholm and they strike up a friendship. In Valdavero she goes to see her old friends Maria and Carlos de Cordobes and their adopted son, Manuel, her childhood sweetheart. But Manuel has vanished in very odd circumstances. Helen becomes involved in the search for him, high in the Andes among the guerrillas who have staged a spectacular kidnapping involving Keith.

Books by Judy Chard
in the Linford Romance Library:

PERSON UNKNOWN
TO BE SO LOVED
ENCHANTMENT
APPOINTMENT WITH DANGER
BETRAYED
THE SURVIVORS
TO LIVE WITH FEAR
SWEET LOVE REMEMBERED
WINGS OF THE MORNING
A TIME TO LOVE
THE UNCERTAIN HEART
THE OTHER SIDE OF SORROW
THE WEEPING AND THE LAUGHTER
THROUGH THE GREEN WOODS
RENDEZVOUS WITH LOVE
SEVEN LONELY YEARS
HAUNTED BY THE PAST
OUT OF THE SHADOWS

JUDY CHARD

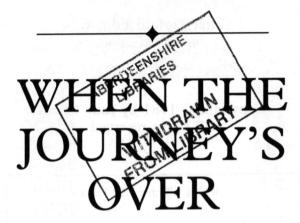

WHEN THE JOURNEY'S OVER

Complete and Unabridged

LINFORD
Leicester

First published in Great Britain in 1981

First Linford Edition
published 2006

Chard, Judy
    When the journey's over.—Large print ed.—
Linford romance library
1. Love stories
2. Large type books
I. Title
823.9'14 [F]

ISBN 1–84617–144–X

Published by
F. A. Thorpe (Publishing)
Anstey, Leicestershire

Set by Words & Graphics Ltd.
Anstey, Leicestershire
Printed and bound in Great Britain by
T. J. International Ltd., Padstow, Cornwall

This book is printed on acid-free paper

1

A warm hand rested on Helen's where it grasped the ship's rail, making her pulses quicken a little at the touch.

'A penny for them!'

Keith Denholm was the kind of person you couldn't help liking — or was she perhaps fooling herself, was what she felt for him more than liking as the result of a casual encounter on board ship? She swung round and smiled up at him.

'The cliché reply is that they are worth much more, but perhaps that's just a matter of opinion!'

He linked his arm with hers and drew her away from the rail, pointing at two chairs which stood side by side on the upper deck where some thoughtful member of the crew had put them.

'Those look lonely without a couple of companions, how about a drink before lunch? We're not due to dock till three o'clock because of the tide.'

As they had called in at various ports down the Pacific coast the passengers had thinned to only a handful, the few left on board the cargo boat, which was due to dock at Valdavero in an hour or so, were excited but a little sad, too, at saying goodbye to new friends they had made among the paying passengers. They had the slightly jaded and dejected air people wear at the end of a voyage. Not that Helen Elliot had mixed much with the others; she and Keith seemed to have gravitated naturally together and enjoyed each other's companionship. The weather had changed as they reached the Humboldt current, the flying fish disappeared and the grey, silent water became blue and choppy. The coastline, too, had changed from rolling green jungle to huge cliffs and an endless line of mountains.

Helen spent a lot of time on deck watching through the haze that always seemed to give land seen from the sea such an air of mystery and desirability as she strained to make out details behind the mist where the Andes soared up like huge teeth against a cloudless sky.

Keith called to a passing steward and ordered two dry martinis. Turning to Helen he grinned. 'I didn't ask you what you'd like; I've got kinda used to making it a couple of martinis about this time of day. O.K?'

'Of course, and thanks.'

They sat down in the chairs and he sighed. 'I'm always sad when a flight or a voyage ends, however short, somehow I'm reminded of the words of the poet Housman when he said 'When the journey's over, there'll be time enough for sleep.' Like him, I hate to miss a moment of what's happening.' He paused a moment, then, 'But thank you for your company; it'll take me a long time to forget this particular trip. In lots of ways it's been special . . . remember that time we went ashore in the Canal zone of Panama? Can't just recall the name, but we took a taxi and when we were driving down that boulevard of flowering trees we suddenly heard a burst of gun fire and then saw that man standing in the garden firing a machine gun at a flower bed. I don't know when I've laughed so much as when the taxi driver said with a completely dead pan face, 'He's just bored, Señor, because it is Sunday!' I've felt the same myself.'

She laughed. 'I know, I was sure some new revolution had broken out. But we forgot all that when we were eating that super lunch in a garden full of orchids with parrots in the trees and the old houses with the canna lilies in the flower beds, those neatly mown lawns running down to the water's edge . . . ' She hesitated. 'I must seem like a little hick to you with all the travelling you've done.'

He smiled down at her. 'I suppose you could say I've served my apprenticeship going around the world working with all the different companies Dad owns, in fact, sometimes I can't remember just where I have been.' He lifted his glass. 'Anyway here's to the future — for both of us.'

She glanced away from him for a moment; thoughts of the future had been something she had shied away from, but now they would have to be faced when she met her father.

As if he guessed something of what was passing through her mind Keith said gently, 'How long since you saw your father?'

'More than ten years — a decade. It feels almost like a lifetime. I can scarcely remember what he looks like to be honest, apart from the photos my mother had.' Her voice broke as she spoke of her mother.

Gently he squeezed her hand.

'Want to talk about it?'

'There isn't much to tell really — as you know, my father is a doctor.'

'Yes, like father like daughter — or should it be the other way round?'

'I suppose I did follow in his footsteps. I'd always wanted to. I adored him as a child. He started as a ship's doctor, I expect on a boat much like this, in the Merchant Navy. He was always away, it seemed, but then he found this tremendous need for medical help among the poor of Boldivia and he simply settled there and set up a practice on the outskirts of the port where we're going to dock, Valdavero.'

'But I think you said he isn't there now?'

'No, it seems he moved out to run a clinic of some kind at the foot of the Andes, about two hundred miles away. It sounds pretty primitive and unhygienic.'

'There speaks the young woman of medicine!' There was only gentle mockery in his voice.

'I know, and it's all so easy when you're in hospital with every facility, but I suppose in a way it's a test of the true doctor to be able to cope without all the aids.'

'And is that what you plan to do, to

go into partnership?'

She shook her head vigorously. 'Heavens, no! I'm just going to stay with him for a while and try to persuade him to come home.'

'In a way we are both in the same position. I'm going to join my father in his business, but I shan't be able to persuade him away from South America; to him it's some kind of paradise.'

'But not for you?'

'It's hard for me to say, I don't really know it. First of all I was away at school and college, since then, as you know, I've been a travelling man. I don't suppose really I know it even as well as you do.'

Keith had told her his father was Nicholas Denholm, an American, originally from Boston, but now chairman and managing director of Denholm Electronics with a big factory complex in Valdavero and branches all over the world. Keith had joined the boat at Florida with huge packing cases of new

7

machinery, delicate instruments and so on; the reason he had taken a slow boat instead of a fast jet, he had told her, and then added, 'And I am grateful to Fate for her vision or I would perhaps not have met you.' His eyes had been warm, gentle, sincere as he spoke, and she had looked away swiftly. She didn't know if she could trust her heart, there was the past and the people in it who would not let her be until she had seen them once more.

'Why do you want him back in England? You haven't got anything against South America, have you?'

'No, of course not. How could I, I don't even know it . . . it's just that it seems such a waste and he's not a young man anyway. He ought to be thinking of retiring and I can't imagine he'll want to live out his days away from home.' The word came out automatically. Always she remembered her mother had kept up the hope, the pretence in a way, that one day Steven Elliot would 'come home'. There had been no violent rift in their marriage, no legal separation between them, it was simply that Helen's mother couldn't take the life. She'd gone to join her husband and lived there for six years, hating every moment of it; the way he usually got paid 'in kind', for his services — chicken and fruit — the people had little money and the life was hard, although Steven became absorbed in it. She always remained apart — a gringo — a foreigner, the term used mostly for English and Americans. She had accepted it with its original sting, a term of contempt. For six years she had lived with it, but then it became just too much, particularly as Steven became more and more caught up with the local people who lovingly called him 'Papa Elliot'. But it was when he decided he was going to move up to the high plateau, the Altiplano where the Andean Indians lived, descendents of the Incas, of the Amyhara whom they had conquered, and of the Spanish Conquistadores . . . it was then Frances

Elliot, usually even-tempered and long-suffering, flared up at last.

The problem of communication alone terrified her. The roads, which seasonal floods could turn into swamps, landslides and sudden storms could destroy them in minutes, and so she had made the final decision and gone, taking Helen with her.

At first the child had felt a deep resentment. She adored her father, and in spite of her mother's dislike of the country, and his absorption with his profession, she had a marvellous childhood — wild, untamed, but completely happy. She had spent most of her time on the plantation of Don Carlos de Cordobes and his wife, Dona Maria. They became like an aunt and uncle to her. Dona Maria's family had owned vast estates and she had brought her fortune to her husband, Carlos. He was like someone from a Spanish painting, dark with flashing eyes and a small imperial beard. his hair streaked with grey which added to his classic looks. Always he dressed immaculately in a pale silk suit with a fresh flower in his buttonhole, and shining brown boots in which you could see your face.

The house had a huge stone gateway with a coat of arms. No one was sure where it had come from, but what did it matter? It lent an air of extra grandeur to the house, entered through a courtyard where an old carriage stood under some trees. Behind it were the stables and loose boxes. Doves cooed and strutted on the roof, through an archway a second fountain stood beneath an almond tree which somehow seemed to Helen always heavy with pink blossom, falling like confetti on the mown grass . . . doorways led into cool, dark rooms where Dona Maria sat and did exquisite embroidery, the walls hung with tapestries, and a shaft of sunlight would catch the diamond rings on her fingers as they moved over her work. When she saw Helen she would hold out her arms . . . 'Chiquitita!'

Along the sides of the room were

window bays with seats in them and curtains to the floor in golden damask, behind which she and Manuel would hide . . . On the walls hung gilt framed mirrors reflecting the furniture and the grand piano with its cover of embroidered silk and the glass chandeliers . . . then there was the garden with orchards, flower borders, lawns, hedges of roses, and a walled area for vegetables and vines. All around were the tilled fields, groves of poplar and cypress, the orchards in bloom.

But above all now as she sat on the deck of the gently rocking ship, she thought of Manuel . . . Manuel of whom she had thought almost continuously down the years; he was also part of the future about which she had been thinking. Manuel with his black hair and skin which looked as though always kissed by the warm sun, his eyes flashing like jet and his teeth white as peeled almonds when he smiled. And Manuel often smiled; he was one of the happiest, most carefree people she had ever known. Maria and Carlos had adopted him. He was the son of one of their foremen. His mother had died at his birth and soon after, his father had been killed by one of the giant tractors that worked Don Carlos' land, so without thinking twice, the Cordobes had simply taken him in. They had no children of their own, and he became their beloved son, it was as simple as that.

So Manuel and Helen had become like brother and sister, inseparable. He taught her to ride, took her fishing, boating on the lake, up on the altiplano. He was her hero, her whole life at thirteen, when the first stirrings of womanhood aroused her, he had perhaps started to become something more than a brother, although to her simple and unsophisticated mind she had not recognized the beginnings of womanly attraction for a man . . .

Now once more she wondered.

All she knew at the time was that when her mother decided to take her back to England where, in her words, she could be 'properly educated', it was as if part of her heart had been wrenched out, as though half of her very being were left in that magic country which had been her home . . .

2

Now she felt Keith's eyes on her, enquiring, but gentle as always.

'I'm sorry, I was woolgathering. It's so odd to come back to a place which once was all one knew of home, and yet in a way not to belong. I shan't know anyone; it will be all strange, and it's bound to have changed so much even from what I remember.'

'Yes, I know. In a way I'm feeling much the same, but are you going up to the altiplano right away, to Malagante — I think that's where you told me your father has his clinic?'

'No, actually I'm staying a couple of nights in Valdavero.' She hesitated and looked away over the sea to the coastline which now was so close she could see the cars and the people on the shore. 'I have some friends I want to visit on the outskirts of the town. They have a plantation.'

He got to his feet and pulled her up towards him.

'That's marvellous, great, you can come to the party tomorrow. Dad's laid on a kind of welcome home with the fatted calf bit for the prodigal.' He pretended to look serious. 'It's going to be a very grand affair from all accounts with local dignitaries, the Governor and so on, but he promised a good band and as I know what a super dancer you are, I think you'll enjoy it.' He paused a moment and then took both her hands in his. 'Besides I want you to meet my folk — my father and mother, and my small brother who I really hardly know, he's only eight.' He grinned. 'A beloved afterthought, Dad calls him, but from what mum has told me in her letters he sounds like a holy terror. Still, probably I was the same at that age.'

'How lovely! Thank you for asking me. I'd really enjoy that.' She realized as she spoke that she had been dreading saying goodbye to this young man with his fair, typically American good looks. He radiated good health and the great outdoors almost as if it were a deliberate image, which she knew it wasn't. For a young man in his position, with his background and wealth, he was natural, unspoilt and unassuming. She knew she was going to miss his company, so the party would be a bonus.

She gave him the Cordobes' phone number. 'They'll take a message if I should be out,' she said as he tucked it into his wallet.

With much shouting and noise, and what appeared to be utter confusion, the boat docked and as she walked down the gangplank she saw a battered landrover standing on the quay nearby. A tall man was getting out and although it was more than ten years, she still recognized that head, like a tawny lion, she had thought as a child. The figure now was a little more stooped, but still towered above the people round him.

'Father!' She knew he couldn't possibly hear her above the din and bustle but the word had burst from her involuntarily. She forgot everything now — Manuel, Keith, even the future as well as the past as she ran forwards and flung her arms round him.

'Nel, my darling child.' He used the childish endearment, bringing the sting of sudden tears to her eyes. He smelt faintly of antiseptic and tobacco, as he always had, and suddenly the years rolled away in the haven of his arms. Then slowly he held her away from him. 'Let me look at you. What a beautiful young lady! I can hardly believe that leggy little girl has turned out such a stunner!'

Swiftly she took in the threadbare tropical suit. It was crumpled but clean, obviously the last thing he was concerned with was appearance, just as he had always been, a dedicated man, something which had irritated her mother almost beyond endurance . . . 'Why can't he be dedicated in a nice

18

clean modern hospital in London?' she had said.

Now Keith came up behind her and she turned.

'Dad, this is Keith Denholm. We've been shipboard companions from Florida.'

Steven held out his hand. 'Nice to meet you, my boy. I don't come to Valdavero much these days, but naturally one hears of your father and his great success.'

For a moment Helen wasn't sure if there was a slight edge to her father's voice, but realizing she hardly knew this man now, she dismissed the idea as quickly as it had occurred.

Keith grinned. 'I'm a stranger in these parts myself, Doc. But I've asked Helen if she'll come to a party Dad's giving tomorrow, I'd be mighty honoured if you'd come, too.'

Steven hesitated a moment and then as if something had made him decide as he glanced at Helen's animated face, he said, 'Thank you, my boy. I'd be delighted.' He turned back to Helen. 'Come along then. I have some medical supplies to pick up so I can drop you off at your hotel.'

'But I thought I told you in my letter, I'm going to the Cordobes,' she said swiftly. For a moment his face was shadowed as he dropped his gaze.

'I see,' he said shortly. 'Well, in that case, we'll go over that side of the town first.' He took her cases and turned on his heel. For a moment she felt snubbed and shivered as if a cloud had covered the sun. She followed him across the quay and climbed into an old jalopy which smelt of leaking fuel, its rusting doors held together with cord. As she did so, she glanced back and saw Keith getting into a chauffeur driven Rolls, his leather cases piled in the boot. He leant forward and waved as her father let in the clutch and they jerked away into the teeming streets beyond the docks.

They passed a half finished luxury hotel on the edge of the sea, its lounges and halls slung out on concrete

20

buttresses over the rocks, with walls of glass to show the view across the blue bay to a line of pink and purple mountains, below them thundered the great Pacific breakers, crashing over jagged little promontories. Thousands of sea birds — white gulls, black cormorants with vicious beaks, wheeled and flapped about in the air.

As they reached the town itself, Helen felt a sudden sadness, she wasn't sure why, nostalgia perhaps. The smell of fish and guano hung over everything, some of the buildings had a quiet kind of dignity, there was an English church, a small square with pepper and eucalyptus trees, a dusty bed of bright zinnias, and benches where old men slept, oblivious of the noise of shoe-shine boys and an old squeaky barrel organ which, for some reason brought an uprush of homesickness for London, although she had never seen one in the streets there.

Her father had been silent, now he said, 'Nel, I'm sorry I couldn't get to

England when your mother died. I didn't get word till it was too late.'

She felt a sudden stab of resentment. All her life in a way she had been pig in the middle, as if she were to blame somehow for her parent's quarrel, her mother always referring to Steven as 'your father' not my husband, and now he was doing just the same thing in reverse. She bit back the retort which had risen to her lips; it was not her business to judge. At the time she had felt a bitterness but now she saw him she could believe not only the remoteness had prevented him receiving the message, but that shortage of funds could have been partly responsible for his absence, both excuses which she had been tempted to ignore at the time.

He patted her knee. 'Not much to do here, Nel. How are you going to keep yourself amused?'

She took his hand with its long, sensitive fingers, hands that had brought comfort to cut knees and bruised limbs, as well as egos, when she had been a child.

'I don't need amusing, I'm a big girl now,' she grinned. She decided she wouldn't bring her guns to bear on the question of his returning to England yet. The excuse she had made for her trip was a short holiday before she took up the junior partnership in a group practice in the suburbs of London she had arranged. 'I hoped to get some practical experience with you, I can't think of a better teacher,' her tone was light and for a moment he didn't answer.

'In this country,' he said at last, slowly, 'to many of the people, the idea of going to hospital is certain death. If you walk in the wards you can believe it. Some of the cases are beyond belief, they are so pathetic. Tiny shrunken inert bodies of old men and women, the terrible silence, the vacant stares lost in pain or numbed by their illness and the unfamiliar surroundings. A man is employed even to keep the dogs from straying in from the streets. It is a constant war against dirt, ignorance, and superstition; things you never have to contend with in England, but they are like children.'

As he spoke she remembered from her childhood the ochre skinned people dressed in parrot feather capes of blue and gold. Some of the magic began to work, but then as if he needed to disillusion her, perhaps to keep her feet planted firmly on the ground, he said, 'In some cases it is kinder to let them live as they wish, on coca . . . '

'Coca?' She wrinkled her brow; she had forgotten.

'The plant from which cocaine is obtained.' He pointed. 'Look there, it's sold everywhere, outside the markets, even on the street corners in the richer part of the town you'll find a coca seller huddled on the ground, the pile of pale grey-green dried leaves like small bay leaves.'

Helen glanced round. There were also piles of peculiar stuff which looked like long strands of black liquorice rolled into coils in icing sugar. 'What on earth . . . ?' She turned to Steve. He looked even more grim.

'They're made from the ash of the quinoa and dried, then mixed with spittal into a sticky mass and shaped into those little cakes, you put them in one side of your mouth and in the other a little pouch of the coca leaves.'

'But surely they must know what it's doing to them!' Her instilled horror of drugs and what they did to the human body made her almost physically sick. He shrugged again. 'To many coca is a necessity, a means to get above life, out of the struggle, away from care.'

He drove slowly as he talked. 'From childhood almost every Indian chews coca, it doesn't bring the hallucination of other drugs, but a kind of tranquillity, a relief from hunger, cold, pain . . . in the ultimate, resignation.'

She sat speechless with horror. And yet in a way it was as if dawn had broken in her mind. Suddenly she could see how, as a doctor, her father had felt he must make an effort, must do something to help these people whom he looked upon as his children, his responsibility.

His face had taken on a greyish tinge as if just talking about it had taken some of the life from him.

'Many people think all the hopelessness and helplessness of the Indians, their indolence and lack of initiative and apparent stupidity are due to coca, but you might as well talk to that wall, you'll never convince them it is so.'

Now they had reached the hacienda of the Cordobes, and all other thoughts were driven from her mind at the anticipation of meeting them. Her father opened the door and helped her out, handing her the cases.

'Aren't you coming in for a moment?'

He shook his head, not meeting her eyes. 'No, I don't want to spoil your . . .' he hesitated a moment, 'your homecoming. I know what feeling you have for Don Carlos and Dona Maria; it is their moment to have you alone.

Tomorrow evening I will come and collect you for the party. Adios, Nel.' He bent and kissed her briefly on the forehead as though she were still a small child, and for a moment she felt as if she were indeed back in those days of childhood when he would drop her at the hacienda on his way to the hospital, those golden days when all that mattered to her was Manuel.

She walked slowly up the drive. An old man was hoeing a flower bed, his back to her. For a moment she stood watching him, containing her mounting excitement with difficulty. Juan had been head gardener at the Casa Cordobes ever since anyone could remember, and she and Manuel had enlisted his help and advice over many of their childish pranks and projects. It seemed he was ageless and now as her shadow fell on the ground, he turned. For a second he scowled and she thought he had forgotten her, or perhaps his eyesight had gone, forgetting how much she had changed. Then suddenly he threw down his hoe, and a huge grin split his face as he said, 'Chiquitita Elliot!'

Without another word or waiting for an explanation, he ran ahead calling for Dona Maria and Don Carlos. She followed him through the pergolas and arches where bougainvillaea and roses grew, jasmine and geraniums, Golden Shower and a creeper whose name she couldn't remember but which seemed everywhere, covering walls and buildings with huge pale purple bells. There were arum lilies, pansies, violets, pinks and nasturtiums, never had she seen such a profusion of colour or smelt such a cloud of perfume . . . she had forgotten how truly lovely it was.

At the sound of Juan's voice Dona Maria came to the big open doors. Although now in her early sixties she was strikingly beautiful, her hair thick and white as snow, swept up on the top of her head, and her eyes were brilliant, the whites almost blue like those of children, and she wore a long soft, pale green dress the colour of the outer husk of an almond.

At first, as she saw Helen, she swayed as though she might faint. The girl ran forwards and took her hands.

'Tante Maria . . . ' always the Cordobes were aunt and uncle . . . now the tears were coursing down her cheeks, still as smooth and delicate as rose petals. She held Helen at arms' length for a moment before enfolding her in a close embrace.

'My child, my darling little one, cherie, chiquitita . . . ' all the endearments tumbled from her, 'we were, of course, expecting you, and yet till you actually came I would not let myself believe it. Carlos told me not to be ridiculous, that you would be here, but . . . ' she looked away a moment, 'perhaps it is because I get old . . . people do not seem to keep their word like once they did, but I should have known with you it would be different.' Releasing her, she took her hand. 'Come, Carlos will never forgive me if I keep you for more than a moment away from him.'

She threw open the door. Helen remembered the room so well, large with perfect proportions and exquisite furniture.

Don Carlos sat in a shaft of sunlight which heightened the golden colours of the room and the brilliance of the crystal. For a moment it was as though the people who had lived there down the years might come in, too, and walk about — she had always felt that — so often Dona Maria had talked of the parties they had once held when they were young . . . 'Fifty people perhaps, come to the fiesta . . . and then stay a month!'

For a moment Don Carlos did not hear them, he was studying papers at his enormous carved desk. He looked more distinguished than ever, for age had lent more classic distinction to his features and the Spanish ancestry was more evident than before. He was still slim as a reed and, as always, dressed in a cream suit of heavy silk, his beautifully trimmed moustache and pointed beard grey instead of jet black, but to Helen he still looked like the picture she had seen of 'El pirata Drake . . . '

Maria spoke his name and he looked up, leaping to his feet and grasping Helen in a bear like hug and she was enveloped in his strong arms, surrounded once more by the perfume of citronella of which he always smelt.

Iced orange juice was brought and put on the marble topped table, a magnum of champagne with tulip shaped, priceless crystal glasses. Dona Maria sank into a low arm chair while Helen sat in one of the large window seats as she had always done. Don Carlos stood with his back to the enormous fireplace piled with logs and cones. It was as if the years between had never been as they all talked at once, asking questions, trying to answer, laughing . . . and yet all the time, inside, she waited, her eyes straying round the room, looking for some sign of Manuel — a book perhaps, some pipes, a magazine . . . but apart from some old photographs of them both when they were children, there was nothing.

At last Dona Maria got to her feet. 'Come, my child, you must want to shower and change. Dinner will not be until half past eight when it is cooler. It is too hot to eat early. That will suit you?'

Helen stooped and kissed her. 'Of course, and please don't make any fuss. I want everything to be just as it always was.'

For a moment a cloud seemed to pass over Dona Maria's face, then quickly she smiled, but the smile didn't reach her dark eyes as she said, 'Nothing can remain the same, my child. Life has to go on, to progress, whether we like it or no.'

Before Helen could think of any reply she had gone, closing the door softly behind her.

The room was luxuriously furnished with a small bathroom leading off. Helen was glad to strip off her clothes and stand under the warm shower, and then to put on fresh underwear, she hadn't realized how hot and sticky she felt.

When she had finished dressing she opened the door softly and peered down the corridor. The house was hushed and peaceful as though everyone slept in the evening heat. Quietly she tiptoed across the landing to the room she knew was Manuel's. There was no reply to her knock so she pushed open the door. Although the bed was made up, and some of his clothes hung in the closet, it had the feeling of emptiness that only an unused room can have, a kind of watchful waiting as though the very furniture itself was in suspended animation till the occupant returned. She felt certain Manuel had not slept there for weeks, perhaps even months . . .

Dinner was a relaxed meal.

'Su casa, my child,' Carlos said. 'It is your home, please do as you wish.' Already she felt part of the house again, as if she had truly come home — apart from the vacant space left by Manuel . . .

They asked about her mother, and were sad to hear she had been ill for so long. She told them of her training in the London hospital, and then at last, unable to contain her curiosity any longer she asked,

'Where is Manuel, Tante Maria?'

There was a small silence during which the bird song outside seemed almost deafening. Someone in the distant kitchen dropped a plate, there was a soft laugh. Helen wondered if indeed Manuel was dead and they had not told her — an accident perhaps . . .

The couple looked at each other down the length of the gleaming polished table with its fine damask, the silver, the crystal goblets and the huge bowl of fragrant flowers, then slowly

Maria nodded at Carlos . . .

He had dismissed the servants, and now he was smoking one of the beautiful cigars he had made for him specially in Cuba, the blue smoke curled upwards in rings to the carved and painted ceiling.

'Three years ago we sent Manuel to America to College — Yale . . . '

Dona Maria lifted her hand in a gentle protest. 'That is not quite right — we did not *send* him, he wished to go.'

Carlos inclined his head in agreement. 'Yes, it is so, he wished to go. He was quite brilliant at school, and he was doing well at the College. Then six months ago, just before he graduated, they wrote to us to ask if he had returned home before the end of the term. We could not understand it, it seems he had simply disappeared from the University, from the campus, no one had seen him go, nothing had been heard of him for several weeks.' His voice broke and he was so overcome with emotion he found it difficult to continue.

Helen waited with ill-concealed impatience. However painful it might be for them all, she had to know.

'We did not know whether to think him dead, kidnapped . . . we checked with Immigration as soon as we could, but as far as they could tell me he had never come back to Boldivia. There was no word, no trace. The police have done all they could, but it is hopeless . . . '

Helen could see they were both broken-hearted, Manuel had been their son, closer perhaps because they had none of their own.

'We did wonder at one time if perhaps he had gone to England . . . ' Dona Maria glanced swiftly at Helen. 'But we could see no reason . . . '

As if for the moment it was too painful to say more, they rose to their feet and Helen followed them into the big sitting room, trying to absorb this astounding piece of information, not in the least what she had expected. It just didn't seem possible someone like Manuel could disappear . . .

The sun was setting behind the town and beyond, in the distance in the brief twilight the Andes soared up like huge teeth against a cloudless sky as a huge silver moon hung above. It filled her with an infinite sadness, mostly because of what she had just heard. It was as if the sun had gone out of her life . . . but for the moment she could not ask more questions, could not probe into their grief . . .

Now they talked of Steve. 'I have not seen 'Papa Elliot' as they all call him, for months,' Carlos said. 'I think he comes only very seldom to the city these days.'

Dona Maria nodded. 'He works too hard that one, drives himself like a mule. How can one possibly criticize a saint, eh?'

Helen nodded. It was on the tip of her tongue to tell them she intended to persuade him to return to England with her, but something made her hold back, this was not the time to talk of partings . . . perhaps that was it.

Later, as she lay in the huge four poster bed with its rose coloured damask curtains, moonlight spilling on to the Chinese carpet, she felt wide awake in spite of being physically drained. She thought of Manuel, of what could possibly have become of him — and of Keith — but most of all of Tante Maria who looked ill, strained, her eyes shadowed and haunted as if they had seen something she did not wish to remember . . .

3

The day passed in talk, in walking through the gardens, in remembering . . . it was difficult though to talk of the past without mentioning Manuel's name and all the time his face, his intangible presence seemed to hang between them all like a shadow, a wraith from the past, so that she was in a way glad when it was time to change for the party.

When Steven arrived he had on a shabby evening suit which looked as though it dated from the days of King George, with a starched shirt and black bow tie; the trousers were too short and he had on blue socks and cracked patent leather shoes, all of which it seemed he had borrowed. Somehow it made Helen want to cry . . . to take him in her arms and croon to him as if she were the parent and he the child.

He was already late so the meeting between himself and the Cordobes was brief, and somehow Helen, sensitive as always to atmosphere, felt it to be strained and stilted as if they were strangers, not old friends.

When they arrived at the Town Hall where the party was to be held, everything else vanished for the moment in her pleasure at the colourful scene, the music, the ceaseless movement of the people. Keith was so pleased to see her and quickly took her and Steven to meet his family, hardly giving her time to speak to them before he whirled her away on the floor to the rhythm of the band, whispering in her ear, 'I thought the hours would never pass till I saw you again . . . '

There were dress uniforms everywhere, glittering ball gowns from New York and Paris, and down one side of the immense hall, a table bearing the most stupendous array of food Helen had ever seen. Briefly she thought of the squalor and poverty her father had described, and glanced round for him. He stood with his arms folded, leaning against one of the window embrasures, apart, aloof, somehow as if he stood in judgment, in his shabby suit. The contrast between him and his poverty — chosen as it might be — with the wealth of the Denholms struck her more forcibly than ever, she even felt a little spurt of annoyance that he should seemingly, deliberately, be spoiling the party for her, but quickly she shook off the feeling, certain nothing could be further from his mind. It must be because everything was so strange, so different . . . and then as they danced in an ever increasing crescendo of movement, suddenly, through the crowd, she saw a man standing with a tray of drinks, waiting to cross between the whirling couples, for a moment their eyes met and her blood ran cold. For a split second she had seen recognition in answer to hers — she was certain of it . . . it was Manuel.

She stumbled in Keith's arms and he

said, 'Sorry love, did I tread on your toes?'

'No . . . it's just . . . oh, it can't be, I'm just imagining things . . . I thought I recognized someone.' They stopped and she pointed to where Manuel had been standing. But there was no one there. 'I was certain I saw him.' She was confused. Could it really have been him? She'd never forget those eyes; they had haunted her ever since the day she and her mother had sailed away for England.

Keith led her back to the table for now the scene was to change. A group was taking over for disco dancing and all was bustle and confusion as she gazed round, trying to catch sight of the man again.

The Governor mounted the stage and called for a moment's quiet as he spoke into the mike. He had a glass in one hand and an eloquent torrent of words fell from his lips as he spoke of the Denholms and of Keith who had 'returned to the fold'. Glasses were lifted, first of all to the President, then to the Queen, and then to Nicholas and his wife and Keith. The band struck up the Boldivian anthem, then a rather shaky version of God Save the Queen, and the Stars and Stripes . . . As the last bars cracked into silence Nicholas was handed the mike and he thanked everyone for their kindness.

'Please forgive us,' he went on, 'we have another son as well as Keith, young Mark, and we think it is time he went to bed.' There was much laughter, then he went on, 'and his mother and I, being the other end of the age scale, are also feeling it is time we left you young people to enjoy yourselves . . . ' There was another round of applause and then the band put up their instruments to make room for the group.

Nicholas came over to where Keith and Helen were standing. 'Please forgive us, Helen, my dear, but Mark is inclined to get over-excited, he is rather highly strung, so keep an eye on Keith for us, will you, and do please call and visit us whenever you can.'

Helen thanked them, said goodbye to Peggy, Keith's mother, and young Mark who was looking sulky at being dragged unwillingly away.

Now people started to drift towards the bar and the buffet and Helen looked round for her father. She felt a little guilty she had been so wrapped up in all the gaiety she had forgotten for the moment that he was alone, but after all this was his home country more than hers and surely he must have friends in the town, even if he actually lived nearly two hundred miles away.

He was still standing where she had originally seen him. She touched Keith's arm. 'May I bring my father over?'

Almost before the words were out of her mouth, he said, 'Of course, I'm sorry, Honey, how thoughtless of me! But when you're with me I find it difficult to think properly.' He squeezed her hand. 'I'll go get him.'

She watched him stride over to where

her father stood. In some ways Keith himself reminded her of how her father had been when she was a child — tall, like a Viking — now Keith towered above him, although probably he wasn't all that much taller. It was obvious her father was taking some persuading. He glanced at her, and she nodded and smiled, indicating the chair by her side. With a little shrug almost of resignation, he turned and followed Keith.

'What will you drink, Doc?'

'Just orange juice, thanks. I have to make an early start, as you know, and the roads to the altiplano need a clear head and a steady hand.'

Keith laughed. 'You can say that again. From what I remember of them they are fit only for mules and llamas.'

A tall man in a uniform Helen didn't recognize stood nearby with a woman as fair as he was dark. Keith took her hand now and led her over.

'This is Señor and Señora da Costa, he is chief of police in Valdavero; a man to keep on the right side of!'

The man laughed. He, too, reminded Helen of a Spanish grandee with his olive skin and dark curly hair, but he was younger than Don Carlos, slim with broad shoulders. She wondered for a moment if he had been involved in trying to find Manuel. The thought of him once more made her glance round, but there was no sign of the man into whose eyes she had looked with recognition.

Señora da Costa was in complete contrast to her husband with the fragile appearance of Dresden china. She held out a beautifully manicured hand.

'You have come to live here, I believe, Doctor Elliot?'

Helen hesitated not wanting to give away her plans in front of her father. 'Well, actually I'm going to help my father, to gain experience.'

'You are so wise.' Mary da Costa was among those who accepted and enjoyed Boldivian life as it was and had no illusions that things in England would be nearly so comfortable. Her husband had been at University in England where they had met — handsome and lighthearted, he had appealed to her at once, and she loved his country. 'I couldn't bear to live in England now with all that ghastly housework. All my old schoolfriends look about ninety!' She fluttered her eyelids and added archly, 'I'm always being told I don't look any older than my own daughter!'

Helen murmured an appropriate reply, but Mary wasn't to be stopped now. 'Slaving over a hot stove and a sink — what's the point? Here I have four servants; why should I do all the menial tasks?'

Helen felt, rather than saw, what expression there must be on her father's face, but as if determined to turn the knife, Mary now spoke to him. 'As a doctor you must see how these people have brought all this disease and misery on themselves, I am sure, with this terrible indulgence in coca, the slipshod way they go about things, the dirt and squalor they live in, more like animals.

It must be so disheartening for someone like yourself.' She gave him a brilliant smile as her eyes rested on Steve's out of date suit, the cracked shoes, all of which obviously proclaimed his own disregard for all she held precious.

Helen saw his eyes smoulder and was frightened there would be some kind of confrontation, but with a little shrug, as if he were used to such criticism and tired of replying to it, he turned away and picked up his glass of orange juice. Mary turned and whispered something in her husband's ear. He smiled and leaned forward.

'Nice to see you back, Keith,' he said. 'Your father will no doubt be glad to have you help him. A great empire he has built up here in Valdavero.'

Keith smiled, unaware of the slight tension. 'I suppose at least you could say he gives employment to a lot of people who perhaps otherwise would have no job, and I'm told he pays good wages, but that's something I'm going to have to discover for myself. He hasn't told me what he thinks I'm worth yet!'

Everyone laughed — except Steve.

'It can't be easy to find workers who are reliable, this I know only too well,' da Costa went on, sipping his pisco and vermouth, the local grape spirit which most people drank. 'Denholms is a very progressive company, the hospital, the new houses built,' he hesitated, 'but we cannot blame the peasants, I suppose, for the number of brats they breed . . . it is sad, but more young people are always leaving the country.'

His voice was drowned in the beat of the disco music, the strobe lights took over from the chandeliers as the twang of the electric guitars and crashing of drums and cymbals filled the air . . .

Suddenly there was a commotion by the door.

A party of police rushed in and came over to da Costa, surrounding him in a circle, waving their arms, all speaking at once in rapid Spanish, the words falling over each other.

Helen saw Keith make an involuntary movement — of course he spoke Spanish — then he dropped his outstretched hands as if in despair, his face white as a pale flower in the unnatural lighting . . . he turned to her, his features haggard.

'What on earth is it?' she asked.

'It's my parents,' he said, 'and Mark . . . they've been kidnapped . . . the car was ambushed as it drove through the suburbs, some shots were fired . . . the police had to withdraw for fear of injuring the family . . .

'Oh, my God!' He covered his face with his hands . . .

4

A girl screamed — the group went on playing, they were used to screaming and to the Guardia Civil — they took no notice, but da Costa, with surprising agility seemed to be up on the stage in one bound. He snatched the mike from the startled singer who was gyrating in time to the guitars, and as he did so, the beat dropped away, the dancers stood for a moment as if transfixed, like figures in a film that has broken, then a babble of voices broke out as da Costa spoke.

'I'm sorry, there has been an accident, but there is no need for panic, the Guardia are only here with a message, not to keep order or make arrests.' He gave the ghost of a smile. 'Please leave the building as quickly and quietly as you can. Mr Denholm has asked me to apologize on his behalf for

51

the breaking up of the reception. Later we will be able to tell you more — at the moment even I myself am not conversant with all the details.'

With a little bow he turned then to the group, told them to pack up their instruments, disconnected the mike and returned to where Keith still stood, his face ashen, Helen holding on to his arm. One or two people eyed them curiously, someone said, 'Car crash, is it?' He shook his head, too dazed and shocked to speak.

'It is rather bad news,' Helen said quickly. 'Do you mind not asking him any more at the moment?'

Actually he was quite unconscious of what went on around him, his brain seemed paralysed and it had passed on a similar message to his limbs. Fortunately they were near one of the emergency exits and Helen managed to half push, half lead him through it to the car park. She had no idea whether he had a car of his own there or if he had come with the family, most likely the latter, so without stopping to enquire, she bundled him into the landrover which her father had parked near the road as if he didn't wish to be near the sleek, expensive cars that clustered round the building.

Steven himself materialised from nowhere. She hadn't seen him in the ballroom when the Guardia arrived — he may have been there but all she could see was Keith's stricken face.

'We'd better follow da Costa to the police station,' he said shortly, as the chief's car swept by with a scream of sirens and flashing lights. 'Any news that filters through will come there first, I don't doubt.'

At last it seemed as if Keith had realized the full impact of the occurrence. He banged his fists down on the seat of the landrover, making clouds of dust rise so that Helen had a fit of coughing which made her eyes water, but he didn't notice.

'The swine, the rotten swine, whoever they may be, taking them and young Mark, only a kid. What have any of them done and to whom? Who are the bastards anyway . . . and why, why, why?'

Helen didn't attempt to answer. She knew no more than he did, and if her father had any ideas on the subject he seemed disinclined to voice them.

Keith's original numbness had now turned to fury as he ranted on. 'I'm at a double disadvantage, I don't know the country, the terrain, and if they're bandits, terrorists, whatever blasted name they go under, then they could hide up in those god damned mountains for years. I'm like a helpless fool!'

Helen took his hand. 'Look, I know at the moment it seems terrible, hopeless. It is ghastly, the shock alone is shattering, but it's pretty certain all they want is money in exchange. They'll be in touch before morning, more than likely, and da Costa seems an efficient kind of chap . . . '

He looked at her now as if he were seeing her for the first time. 'I wish I had your acceptance, but perhaps if it was your parents . . . ' he broke off and glanced at Steven, 'your young brother, you wouldn't be so calm.'

She looked away at the passing streets and said quietly, 'I know, I'm sorry, but words at a time like this are pretty useless anyway.'

He squeezed her fingers. 'I'm sorry, Helen, I don't know what got into me. I can only say I'm half out of my mind. Just arriving home, and then this happening, it's like an evil kinda dream. God knows I wish it was then I might have some chance of waking up to sanity.'

At last Steven spoke. 'Do you wish me to take you to the police station or do you think it would be wiser for you to go home and wait, in case the kidnappers get in touch there?'

Keith dropped his head on his hands. 'God knows, I don't.'

'Let's go to the police station first and see what da Costa thinks. If he says it would be wiser to go home then we can take you there,' Helen said.

Keith nodded. 'All right, and thanks. In all the classic cases like this it is usual for the relatives to want the police left out of it, but it seems they are in it whether I like it or not.'

'Well, I suppose usually that's because it's done without the police being present, obviously, but we don't know the full details yet. It must have been sheer chance they ambushed them, if that is what they did, in full view of the police.'

Da Costa was attempting to talk on two or three telephones at once, the station was a hive of activity. It wasn't every day its richest and most famous family got kidnapped. Helen felt more confused than ever, and suddenly desperately tired so that even moving her limbs was an effort.

Suddenly she remembered the Cordobes would be expecting her back for the night. It seemed impossible to use any of the telephones in the police station. She turned to Steven.

'Do you think you could go and let Tante Maria know that I shall stay with Keith for a little while, at least until there is some news? I would not like them to worry.'

He nodded. 'I was going there in any case.' For a moment the words did not sink in, in fact it wasn't until later that she realized the impact of what he had said . . .

Da Costa told them that barriers had been put up on all the roads that led out of Valdavero. 'There are many patrols as well, Señor. I am sure we will catch them very soon. They cannot go far. The car has already been found — your father's car — on the outskirts of the town.' He paused a moment. 'It had been burned to a shell, but do not worry, it was thoroughly examined, no one was inside it. It seems strange, it was the flames in the night sky which alerted the police car and when it got there the kidnappers were just driving off. That is when the shots were fired.'

Keith looked more mystified than

ever. 'It sounds as though it was a pretty amateur affair. I can't for the life of me see the purpose.'

'We shall know very soon, I am sure, Señor.' Da Costa lifted yet another phone on his desk which was buzzing like an angry and frustrated bee. Helen sank on to a bench which ran along the wall. The paintwork was a hideous shade of green — garish — with brown woodwork and bright strip lights from the ceiling which made everyone look as though they were suffering from some form of anaemia, draining the colour from lips and cheeks. She leant her head back and closed her eyes for a moment.

Suddenly da Costa gave a shout, a police sergeant came running from the next room. 'Señor, señor! A boy has taken a parcel into the police station, the small one on the road to Malagante . . . '

Helen got to her feet. That was the name of the village where her father had his clinic. 'When they opened it,' the man continued, 'they found a cassette inside, but the duty officer there has no recorder to listen . . . it is from the kidnappers . . . '

Da Costa waved his hand impatiently, interrupting the man in the middle of the spate of words which tumbled from him.

'Get it here at once, man, at once, without delay.'

Steaming mugs of coffee were brought. Helen gulped hers gratefully; her mouth was parched. Some colour had returned to Keith's cheeks and he was talking to da Costa. The anger had subsided a little, a natural reaction to shock, her medical mind told her, and a good safety valve; much better than holding it all in and putting on a brave front, a stiff upper lip, like an Englishman probably would. Americans were inclined to be more volatile, more emotional. But she knew he must be worried sick and with reason as all the other kidnappings sprung to mind — the Hearst case in America — the more recent one in Sardinia . . . everywhere in the world now it seemed kidnapping had followed on the mania for hi-jacking. Wearily she wondered why people couldn't live simple lives at peace with each other . . .

At that moment a man who was obviously a despatch rider in helmet and leather gear, dashed up to da Costa with a small parcel. A tape recorder stood on the desk, and the whole area became suddenly hushed as he slipped the cassette into the slot and switched on.

There was a moment's pause while the tape gave a hiccup, a false start, then someone said — 'Señor, the volume . . . ' With a gesture of impatience da Costa turned up the knob and suddenly a voice said . . .

'Señor Denholm . . . Keith Denholm . . . this message is addressed to you from the People of Boldivia's Rescue Mission. It is for the poor, the downtrodden, the exploited, many of whom work for your father, a capitalist,

who bleeds the poor people white.'
Helen glanced at Keith: his face was taut, his mouth a hard line, a small muscle twitched in his cheek. She could see his fists were tightly clenched at his sides as he murmured, 'Why don't the bastards get to the point?'

There was a moment's pause while the tape ran on silently as if the speaker referred to a sheaf of papers which could be heard rustling.

'We have your parents and your brother. At the moment they are safe, but they will not be returned to you until you have fulfilled to the letter what we ask — and if you do not, their fate will be on your head and yours alone, so listen carefully. Food and clothing to the value of five million American dollars is to be distributed among the poor in Boldivia, the money is to come from Denholm Electronics . . . For the time that is all. There will be further instructions later as to the rendezvous for the drop, so I suggest Señor Denholm that you set about arranging to find this sum of money and buy the goods so the whole matter may be dealt with speedily. The sooner we get what we ask the sooner your family will be returned to you.'

Once again the tape ran on with only surface noise. Da Costa snapped it off. For a moment there was silence, then Keith turned to the policeman.

'What are the chances? I want the truth.' His voice now was expressionless.

Da Costa shrugged. 'I would say fairly good. They sound like idealists. If they were thugs then they would simply demand cash for themselves. If they mean it is simply food and clothing for the poor — then the chances are good.'

'And what if I refuse to pay, to bow to their blackmail, which, however you look at it it is . . .'

Da Costa got to his feet frowning. 'There can be no question of paying, Mr Denholm, I want that clear from the first. No bargaining. If once we start to bow to terrorism then we breed up more terrorism. Besides if they mean to . . . ' he hesitated, dropping his gaze from Keith's keen look. 'I'm sorry, but whether you pay or not will make little difference . . . '

5

Helen climbed wearily into the land-rover. She had managed to persuade Keith to go home and try to get some rest.

'There's nothing you can do, and it won't help if you're crocked up. Da Costa will get in touch with you as soon as he hears anything. Do you want me to come with you?'

He shook his head. 'No, I know you have commitments, and you have been wonderful. I don't know what I should have done without you.' He bent and kissed her gently on the lips. 'But what a home-coming!'

Steven drove through the dark streets. Somehow Helen had thought it must be dawn, but the sky was still like black velvet, bright with millions of stars, the streets alive with patrols of the Guardia Civil. Up from the invisible sea the wind moaned and brushed her face with a kind of tepid dampness, and there was the thick, unidentifiable sweetness of tropical flowers.

They didn't talk much. Her father looked exhausted, old, drawn. She rested her hand on his knee, just as she had done as a child. For a brief moment he covered it with his own, but still he didn't look at her. He seemed deeply preoccupied.

The Cordobes had gone to bed, leaving a note with strict instructions that they were to be awoken when Steven and Helen returned, but they let them sleep on. Dawn wasn't far off, time enough then to tell them the latest news. Helen knew she wouldn't sleep for the few hours left. She showered and changed into slacks and a tee shirt.

Breakfast was a subdued meal, no one seemed in the mood for talk. It was difficult to find a subject. Don Carlos asked Steven about his clinic, and told them Dona Maria was tired and had asked for a tray to be taken to her room. She'd like to see Helen as soon as she had breakfasted.

She went up directly she'd finished her orange juice and coffee, which was all she could face. She felt to try to eat would choke her.

Dona Maria was propped up in the huge four poster, her white hair a cloud about her shoulders, but Helen was shocked by her face, it was almost as if she had aged overnight. She went swiftly to her side and took her hand. It was fragile as a bird might be, she could feel the bones through the flesh.

She lifted it to her lips. 'Tante Maria, you need to rest. Why don't you go away, take a holiday?'

The woman smiled, shaking her head gently. 'I am well, just tired.' She turned her head away from Helen's gaze. 'I miss him Helen.' A tear ran down her cheek and dropped on Helen's hand, catching the shaft of sun which shone through the window. 'Not to know is terrible, even perhaps to know he was dead would be better.'

For a brief second Helen wondered if she should tell Dona Maria of what she thought she had seen last night at the party, but it was too nebulous a thing to recount and might raise her hopes falsely. She intended as soon as she could to do some detective work on her own account to find Manuel . . . How she was not yet sure . . .

'Come back and see us soon, chiquitita . . . ' Maria drew the soft pink shawl round her shoulders as Helen bent once more to kiss her. Steven was calling from below.

'I must go, but I'll come back just as soon as I can.'

They called in at the police station before they left town. Keith was back again, changed into slacks and a sweat-shirt, his face haggard from anxiety and lack of sleep. He was smoking cigarette after cigarette, lighting a fresh one from the butt of the old one. She remembered him as being only a very moderate smoker on board ship. He took her hands.

'I'm afraid the news is not good. Reports have come in that the guerillas have got away to the mountains, which is exactly what I feared. All we can do is wait — blasted well wait. I never was much good at the 'patience-on-the-monument' bit, but it's hopeless to try and look in those mountains without some kind of lead.'

He ground out yet another half-smoked cigarette in the over-flowing ash tray.

'I wish I could stay but I know you have many friends here, at least your family has, and I must go with father to Malagante.'

He tried to smile. 'I know, bless you. I've asked too much of you already. I can't thank you enough for all you did last night.' He kissed her gently on the brow. 'I'll be in touch just as soon as I hear anything.'

The town was starting to wake up slowly as they drove through the streets, in the suburbs olive trees grew among modern villas, squat Indian servant girls hurried to market with their long black plaits swinging behind them. Here and there a gardener watered the green lawns and beds of tropical lilies in the shade of eucalyptus trees and blood red poinsettias. The pavements were dusty and unswept, most of the shops still barred with shutters of dark grey steel and the few people about somehow looked drab and morose. Helen told herself she was tired, her vision distorted.

Now she could see the massive outlines of the Andes against a kind of bluish suffusion of the sky with a layer of mist clinging low over the land. She tried to talk to Steven, but he, too, seemed in a non-communicative mood. As they left the town they drove beside a winding river where Negro labourers loaded gravel into builders' trucks, women thumped clothes in shrunken pools, scrawny dogs and ragged children wandered everywhere; but soon they reached open farmland with lettuce-green vegetable fields and golden vineyards among the reedy lanes of irrigation ditches, and the tall maize waving soft yellow tassels in the breeze that blew up from the Pacific. And then above the arable land the grass ran like sunlight up to the grey crags against the light filled sky. She began to see what her mother had meant by this uncivilized country that God seemed to have forgotten . . . then twenty miles up the valley the sky cleared and the morning sun made the air shimmer over the coloured fields and pylons marched over the blunt hills, the most barren looking hills she had ever seen.

Steven turned to her as if she had spoken her thoughts aloud.

'You could say there is no need for archaeologists to reconstruct the past here; it lives all around you, and I expect you'll think us very primitive, Nel. I have to do the best I can with the least, but I shan't be hurt if you don't want to stay. Much as I love to have you with me, it wouldn't be fair to expect you to give up your valuable training in such a place.' He paused. 'Many people think I am a nutter fighting a losing battle, I know, but until you know these Latin American countries and the people, like I do, it is difficult to appreciate the terrible gulf between the pointlessly rich and the unnecessarily poor. That is the way I see it.'

'Yes, I realize that.' She hesitated a moment. 'As a matter of fact, you did make it rather obvious at the party.'

'I know, I'm sorry. I suppose it was unforgivable.' He stopped, as if he had been about to add something and then changed his mind. 'I'm sorry, I was rather preoccupied. It's difficult, too, for someone fresh from England to understand the position, and it's people like Mary da Costa, who should know better that make my blood boil; people who employ small boys to carry their briefcases through the city streets, even quite small parcels, menial tasks at starvation wages, that is what sticks in my craw.'

The journey in the old vehicle over

the appalling roads seemed never ending. Helen ached in every muscle and joint, but at last Steven said, 'This is it, the beginning of Malagante.'

She looked round with mounting horror at the straggling, overgrown village with its grey stone shacks roofed with corrugated iron, thin with rust, weighted down with boulders, she imagined because of the high winds. The rough pastures were scattered with lichen-green rocks, a pack train of llamas stepped slowly along the road, a heron flew, white against the intense blue of the sky and away in the distance, wheeling and gliding on the thermals, the first condors she had ever seen.

Malagante was one of the makeshift settlements that had sprung up along the roads when they were built, and now time seemed to have passed them by. Garbage was cast behind the houses in untidy heaps where the vultures searched and squabbled.

The landrover stopped with a squeal

of brakes. The houses seemed simply to be glorified adobes with various extensions added on at will, like a Heath Robinson drawing. Some were built of rough local stone like an English cob cottage, some simply of cane bound together and thatched. A solitary llama stood by the gate, motionless. It seemed to gaze at her with a look of mingled disdain and interest through its long lashed eyes. Helen had only ever seen one so close before in a zoo and its expression reminded her of a camel she had once ridden in Regent's Park.

As they went up the steps that led to a small verandah running along the front of the house, a woman came to the door, wiping her hands on her apron. Helen supposed she was an Indian, either Amymara or Quechua, she had a bright blue woven skirt and boots, a coloured bandana and bright golden rings in her ears. Blue black curls peeped here and there from the bandana, her eyes were huge, dark and somehow, sad.

'Buenos dias, Señor Doctor. I expected you earlier.' There was mild reproof in her tone, but a tinge of resignation also, as though it were nothing unusual.

Steven said wearily, 'I know, and I am sorry, Josefa, many things held me up as always.' He turned and put his arm round Helen. 'This is my little girl.' He grinned. 'Grown somewhat since I last saw her!'

Josefa smiled at Helen. 'I can see who is her father,' she said softly and it was obvious from her attitude that 'El Papa' was the apple of her eye and that at least she probably tried to spare him all she could.

The furniture in the house was sparse and shabby, the grey green walls stained with damp, the shutters half drawn against the heat of the afternoon sun. Brown linoleum covered the floor in patches, there were huge worn leather armchairs which Helen remembered vaguely from childhood. One or two faded photos stood on a table, of Helen as a child with her mother . . .

In the small kitchen much evidence of 'payments', as her mother had called them, her tone scornful as she looked at the chickens, half plucked, corn on the cob, potatoes — always potatoes — and a jar of homemade wine called chicha.

Steven led the way into the dispensary and the primitive consulting room with its hanging diagram of letters and figures for testing eyesight, a varnished table with two chairs drawn up, a horsehair examination couch, and a glass cupboard of drugs, pitifully half full. In one corner stood an old roll top desk she remembered, too, from childhood, with a little secret drawer where her father had kept the silver coins he gave her when her first milk teeth came out, telling her the fairies had put them there . . . Papers, forms, certificates, books and letters lay scattered everywhere.

He put his arm along her shoulder. 'This is where I work, Nel. I know what you are thinking, but remember that modern European pharmacy is largely indebted to the discoveries of Peruvian Indians, but now the 'curanderos' regard herbal medicine as only secondary; sympathetic magic is really the basis of their healing, and who can argue with that? Their profession is feared and honoured, in fact it is almost a cult . . . something else we must be prepared to tolerate.'

'I see, and I also see you are still being paid in kind and not cash. Oh, Father, why do you do it?'

He shrugged, turning away. 'What do you suggest? They have no money, as I told you. We manage, we eat at least, and drink a little . . . '

At that moment the telephone jangled.

'Ah, it is working. That at least is something; most of the time the lines seem to be down.' He lifted the receiver and Helen could hear an agitated voice the other end. She sat on the table swinging her legs, watching him. He looked exhausted, frail, in spite of his size, and she noticed his hand shook as he made some notes. She would give him a thorough examination at the first opportunity. Maybe that way she could persuade him to leave this dreadful place. It was even worse than she had anticipated.

He replaced the receiver. 'Now that really is filthy luck; it's the next village, quite a distance away. I have to take some insulin, they've run out. It may mean staying overnight, my lights are non-existent. I meant to get another battery when I was in Valdavero.' He looked away once more, unable to meet her eyes. 'But I forgot . . . oh, well, I have managed before but it isn't worth risking the roads by night. I am so sorry, my dear, but I shall return as early as possible in the morning. Josefa will give you a meal and I have no doubt you will be only too glad to sleep; you must be exhausted.'

In spite of the fact that electricity pylons crossed the hills nearby it seemed, for some peculiar reason known only to such a country, and typical of the unevenness with which civilization had spread, the cables had not been brought down to the village and Josefa cooked on a battery of Primus stoves.

The Indian woman showed Helen her room, which filled her with fresh horror. The stained walls, the window which had obviously had the glass blown out and roughly mended with a double sheet of polythene, which flapped in the breeze. A lumpy bed, a table with a spotted swing mirror and a few pegs in the wall with a brightly coloured curtain across. For some reason the ceiling was covered with wire mesh from which spiders and dead flies hung; she could hear water dripping incessantly in the dark shower compartment which led off.

The dining room had an earthern floor, and in the middle stood a round table with a gaudy oilcloth cover and on this Josefa placed a well seasoned dish of lamb and rice, which was surprisingly good, a bowl of oranges and a fresh pineapple, a bottle of chicha and some terrible coffee. At first she had been disinclined to talk, but at last in her halting English she spoke to Helen.

'El Papa, he is saint, he work too hard,' she shook her head, 'all hours, he never say no. Only last week before he go down to Valdavero to meet you, they bring, in the middle of the night, Indian woman on a litter, her child half born and already dead. The storm was terrible, but he save her life of course.'

It was clear Josefa loved Steven in her own protective way.

Helen took her coffee out on to the verandah where a couple of rotting rattan chairs stood. The blue of the sky was darkening and already the daylight was becoming transmuted into the cold luminescence cast by the rising moon. The fragrance of datura seemed to thicken as the evening shadows length-ened, and the wind was rising, groaning drearily in the tree tops near at hand. Invisible birds started to call and as dusk closed in, the frogs, the toads and the insects began their chorus, which she supposed would become part of her life now . . . The mountains were dense silhouettes against the pale, steel blue sky and a large clumsy bat brushed her cheek so she gave a small involuntary exclamation.

Josefa came from the kitchen, rolling up her apron. 'I am going now, Señora. You will be all right till morning, my house is only a small distance away.' She pointed down the mud road where the small houses and huts were softened now by the silver of moon-light.

For some reason Helen, who had never minded solitude, felt a moment of panic, a coldness as if, as she had said as a child, a goose walked over her grave. Don't be ridiculous, she told herself. A grown woman, a fully qualified doctor . . .

'Of course, I shall be fine, and thank

you, Josefa,' she said aloud. 'I'll see you tomorrow.' She turned and went back into the house. It smelt of antiseptic, dry leaves and decay, making her shiver once more . . .

6

She took some while to get to sleep, then when she dropped off, she dreamed — of violence, of terror, of being unable to move in the path of some terrible horror that moved inevitably nearer. She cried out in her sleep and awoke, clawing her way up through the mists of unconsciousness . . .

Someone somewhere was banging on a door, shouting.

She got out of bed, hardly aware yet of where she was. She pulled on her dressing gown; it was bitterly cold.

For a moment she hesitated. Who on earth could it be at this time of night, or early morning? Someone perhaps who knew she was alone in the house, but even as she stood, uncertain, her hand on the rusty bolt, the thumping on the door was renewed and a man's voice shouted.

'Señor, Papa Elliot, please to open the door, it is urgent . . .'

She pulled it open, recoiling as she did so. The man who stood on the verandah was enormous; he looked like something from a nightmare with his forage cap pulled down over his eyes, a huge red beard seeming to cover most of his chest, and he wore stained and torn battle dress in the standard camouflage pattern which seemed to be uniform all over the world. Behind him, with its engine running, she could see an ancient jeep, still bearing the white star of the American forces. Dimly she could make out two more figures.

'What do you want?'

'El Papa, the doctor, at once. A man is dying. Mortally wounded.' For the first time Helen noticed the automatic rifle in his hand. She hesitated, reluctant to let him know she was alone in the house.

'My father, the doctor, is not here. He was called away urgently, to the next village. I am afraid I do not know the name. Can it wait till tomorrow?'

The man looked stricken. 'Then who are you, señora?'

'I am his daughter. If it is urgent then I will come. I am a doctor, too,' she said slowly, reluctant to get involved.

At once his expression changed. 'Good, come then. It is O.K.'

With trembling hands she drew on slacks and shirt, stuffed medical supplies into an old black bag of her father's she found on the surgery floor. The supplies she could find were pitiful, at best — morphia, disinfectant, some penicillin and dressings. She had no idea how badly wounded the man was. She was about to slam the door behind her when she went back into the bedroom and picking up her pyjamas and handbag, stuffed them, too, into the case. She had grabbed an old duffle coat of her father's to wear over her thin slacks and shirt.

The dew dazzled now on the long tips of the stunted eucalyptus tree by the gate, the air was bitingly cold. Pale streaks of dawn lay behind the mountains.

She climbed into the back of the jeep and hardly waiting for her to sit down, the driver let in the clutch with a bang and they jerked away, throwing up a cloud of dust behind them — towards the mountains.

Soon the road became no more than a dirt track, scooped and gouged by the rains, barely wide enough for a single vehicle. It climbed the steep wall of the valley in a series of hairpin bends so that Helen closed her eyes and prayed nothing would be coming the other way. The edge looked so insecure she could imagine them crashing far down into the valley if they touched it.

Once she asked if they would tell her where they were going, what kind of wound it was their comrade had suffered, but they simply said, 'It is not far. You will see when you get there Señor doctor.'

They spoke quietly. Most of what they said she could not understand. It could have been some kind of local Spanish patois, or perhaps Quechua, she only half listened, until suddenly it was as if an iron fist had clenched her spine, making her blood run cold for from the few words she did understand, this was part of the guerilla band who had kidnapped the Denholms . . . she heard their name mentioned over and over again, and it seemed it was their leader, a man they referred to as Ortega or 'Paco', which she knew meant the Kid — who had been wounded in the raid. The words 'caudillo' — hero or leader — and 'machismo' the pride in masculinity, recurred and it was obvious their leader was a force to be reckoned with, someone upon whom they looked almost with reverence and worship.

The one who had come to the door, he of the red beard, sat with her in the back, his rifle across his knees. She was certain it was loaded. She hoped he wasn't the trigger happy kind. She had found out his name was Flores, but whether his first or second name she didn't know.

When they had been travelling for about an hour a Thermos of hot coffee was passed from mouth to mouth. They offered it to her and suppressing her feeling of revulsion at their filthy hands and clothes, she accepted the strong, bitter liquid for she felt as if her very blood was freezing in her veins.

It was almost dawn now, the air fresh like Alpine air, soft brownish green grass mantled the huge slopes and she wondered if she would soon be affected by soroche — the mountain sickness which could make people unused to it suffer nose bleed, dizziness or even fainting, but so far she felt nothing but a strange invigoration, almost elation.

She gazed through the cracked window of the ancient torn hood which had somehow survived the wind and rain and saw what she imagined must be a disused mine of some kind, a jumble of corrugated iron buildings clambering up a cliffside reflected in the mirror of a tiny lake. No wonder she had heard there was an area like this called the Hills of the Moon . . . it would have been difficult to imagine a more stark ugliness than was spread before her now.

And then suddenly she was more terrified than she had ever been in her life for she realized if this was indeed the guerillas' hide out, then it was hardly likely once she had seen it they would allow her to leave . . . or to live to tell the tale. The mine was obviously derelict, probably worked out or abandoned for lack of money or labour. There were rusting rail tracks with one or two rotting freight trucks, some on their sides, in the centre stood a huddle of tin roofed shacks clustered round the old pit head winding gear, stark against the blue sky. No smoke came from the hut chimneys, no sound of machinery, no sign of life . . .

The jeep stopped and she was bundled out in front of one of the huts. Flores opened the door and the younger man who had driven the jeep pushed past him.

'Ortega?' It was half query, half a plea, as if he begged the owner of the name to answer and reassure.

The room was in total darkness, heavy felt covered the one window, roughly nailed to the frame. Flores held an oil lamp above his head. There seemed to be no furniture other than a single bed which stood near the fireplace in which a few wet sticks smouldered, filling the room with acrid smoke but no warmth.

'Could we have the window open a little, or at least the covering off?' she asked Flores, for he seemed the leader of the party.

He shook his head. 'No, it is not possible.' He pushed her forward as one might a reluctant child.

A man lay on the bed. Helen could just make out a mass of black hair, a pale face with a dark shadow of stubble, sweat gleaming in the flickering lamp light.

Flores pulled back the covers, gentle as a woman now. The rough grey blanket was stiff, soaked with dried blood, dark blood. There was a jagged wound in the stomach. Helen's heart sank. She doubted if anything but an Intensive Care Unit of the most modern type could save this man, but opening her bag she took out the few instruments and supplies she had brought.

'I must have hot water, clean rags, and more light,' she said sharply, as professionalism took over from any other feelings she might have had for the moment.

As if he were used to taking orders, Flores reappeared shortly with a moderately clean earthenware bowl full of steaming water which she filled with disinfectant, gently she wiped away as much of the caked blood as she could, probing with her fingers, thankful the man was deeply unconscious. The bullet was still embedded in the flesh.

'Bring the lamp closer, give me more

light,' she snapped.

Flores moved the lantern above the head of the man on the bed so that nebulous shadows swam like fish on the ceiling as it swung to and fro. The face of the man came into sharp relief in the harsh light. She gasped. The forceps fell from her fingers as her hand flew to her mouth and she uttered the one word . . .

'Manuel!'

7

The shock of seeing Manuel's face in the lamplight momentarily deprived Helen of her cool professionalism — something upon which in the past she had always prided herself.

She put out her hand to support herself, and the feel of the cold metal of the iron bedstead beneath her fingers brought her back to reality.

Quickly she bent and picked up the scalpel, putting it in the bowl of boiling water Flores had brought. She felt his eyes on her and glanced up at him. She didn't know quite what she had expected — derision, contempt, plain dislike perhaps — but there were none of these. There was compassion, almost as a parent might have had for a sick child as he stood looking down at Manuel. She realized he must have thought she had dropped the instrument because of the horror and hopelessness of the injury he had received.

He said shortly, 'Make him well!'

Speaking more to herself than him, she said softly, 'I don't think it's quite so bad as one might suppose from the amount of blood he has lost.' Somehow it helped to speak thus, to try to reassure while she sorted out the turmoil of her emotions. What could it mean? Manuel, Ortega, Il Paco, the Kid . . . all these she had heard him called, the leader of the guerillas. The gentle quiet boy she had once known, the beloved companion. This was not he, could not be . . .

At once she thought of Dona Maria — did she know or had she guessed somehow part of what had happened? Was that what she had looked so sad about, why she had wished almost that she had heard he was dead?

She probed the wound gently, thankful to have something upon which to concentrate, thankful that at least

Manuel was still deeply unconscious.

She managed to remove the bullet. The bleeding had eased a little. She swabbed out the wound, put on a dressing which she had brought in the bag, and pushing the short curls back from her face, turned to Flores. She pointed at the window.

'The window . . . open it. We must have air, at the same time we need heating. I must be able to boil water.'

Flores, if he understood, gave no sign, his eyes still on Manuel.

At that moment, from the corner of her eye, Helen saw the door slowly opening. Her heart quickened its beat. She didn't know what she expected — the whole situation was so bizarre, nothing would have surprised her now, even to be taken out and shot if the guerillas thought Manuel was not so ill as they had anticipated, or if she seemed to have done all she could for him and was now of no more use — she had no illusions on that point. She was expecting another member of the gang, as she thought of them, but as the figure advanced into the circle of light thrown by the lamp she saw it was a woman, little more than a girl, in her late teens, she guessed. She came swiftly, quietly, over to the bed, moving with the grace of an animal. Then she turned to Helen.

'I had heard a woman had been brought instead of El Papa. It is not good. You are medico, Señora? Trained . . . ?'

Helen nodded. 'Yes I am trained, fully qualified,' she said with a tinge of sarcasm.

The girl turned and leaning over the bed said softly,

'Mi amor . . . Ortega . . . it is I, Juanita . . . '

'I'm afraid he can't hear you, Señorita,' Helen said shortly. 'He is deeply unconscious, mostly through lack of blood; the wound itself is hardly more than a flesh wound.'

'He will live?

'Yes, I think I can say he will live

. . . but he would have a much better chance if he could be got to a hospital.'

Even in the poor light Helen could see the girl was breathtakingly beautiful. Even the hideous uniform of bomber jacket, jeans and leather boots, couldn't disguise that. Her face a perfect oval, the lustrous dark hair swept up and pushed in the peaked cap, her eyes a clear bright blue, compelling in their gaze.

'I had heard a woman had been brought, that El Papa was not available, but Manuel . . . his life matters more than anything — to others as well as me.' Her voice was husky with a slight accent.

'I am Steve Elliot's daughter, Helen.'

The girl inclined her head. 'I see. El Papa would save his life, of course. He can work miracles.' She turned now to Flores who still stood at the foot of the bed, his eyes fixed on Manuel, his hands hanging loosely at his sides as if he didn't know what to do with them. His gun lay on the floor. For a moment

Helen's gaze rested on it, but as if he sensed what she might be thinking, he picked it up and turned towards the door. Juanita took his sleeve.

'We must find El Papa. He must be brought.'

For a moment Helen was puzzled, was it that these people knew her father by repute, or that he had at some time attended them when they were ill or wounded?

Slowly an idea started to worm its way into her mind, but it was so preposterous, so unbelievable she dismissed it. She was overwrought, letting her imagination run away with her because of the position she found herself in.

'Just a moment.'

Juanita and Flores swung round at the sharpness of her tone.

'I realize it is you who are responsible for the kidnap of the Denholms last night, I wish to know what has happened to them, where they are and whether they need medical attention.

One of them is a small boy and the other a woman, none of them used to the altitude; it could be harmful.'

Flores looked as if he were about to say something and changed his mind. The girl simply gave her a long, cool look, and turning, walked out of the hut, closing the door softly behind her.

Helen managed to wash some of the blood and dirt from her own hands now she had done all she could for Manuel. Flores had brought more water at her request. She went across to the bed. Manuel was still deeply unconscious, but his breathing and pulse were easier. She turned to the window, lifting the felt that covered it and peered out. The sun now was dazzling above the mountains. She saw the derelict huts all round the small compound where men hung about, dark skinned and dark eyed, she couldn't say how many . . . most of them seemed to be armed with automatic rifles. She thought about the labourers in such mines as this who had died like flies, of accidents, of dysentry and the gnawing verrugas fever of the Andes, something which could attack them all. The expression lunar starkness was aptly descriptive of the scenery.

She turned from the window, dropping the greasy felt over the aperture, and as she did so, the door opened once more. This time it was a man who entered in paramilitary uniform, a gun on his belt. He seized her roughly by the arm. 'Come!'

She tried to draw away, to protest, but he dragged her through the door, past the guard who stood there, his rifle in his hand. She still struggled.

'I cannot leave my patient. He may regain consciousness at any moment!'

The man took no notice, simply tightened his grip on her arm, his nails biting into her flesh, making her wince with pain. He pulled her roughly across the compound to another hut and rapped on the rotting wood of the door. It opened as he did so and she was pushed inside. To her sun dazzled eyes it seemed pitch dark. She put out her hand to steady herself, but it simply met empty air. She could see a thin pencil of light across one window which obviously had shutters drawn and then gradually as her eyes became more accustomed to the dark, what she had thought was emptiness became even more menacing as she saw the silhouette of a man in the shadows in front of the window. He was sitting at some kind of rough table apparently with his back to her. Suddenly without turning, he spoke.

'So, a woman doctor, eh?' He spat on the floor, making her recoil. His voice filled her with terror and a cold kind of despair.

As if he didn't expect any comment from her he went on, 'You have looked at our wounded leader?'

'Yes.' Her voice was hardly above a whisper.

'He will live?'

'If he was taken to an Intensive Care Unit there would be no doubt of that.

He needs plasma, saline drips, the kind of equipment only to be found in a city hospital.'

'Then perhaps it would please the señora doctor if we booked him a suite at the hospital in Valdavero, si?' His voice was heavy with sarcasm making Helen long to hit back, to retort, but she was beginning to learn such behaviour didn't pay. When she didn't answer he went on, 'It will be long before he regains consciousness?'

She was tempted to evade the question, to give as little help to these people as possible, wondering what effect Manuel's recovery would have on the Denholms . . .

'That I cannot say,' she said. 'He is very weak as I have just told you, he needs special attention and drugs. Without them I cannot be responsible for his condition.'

'I think you will find it wise to be responsible, Señora,' he barked at her, turning slowly round, and in the dim light that filtered through the shutters she could see his eyes glinting as he turned up the flame of a paraffin lamp that stood on the floor. She guessed he was a cholo, stocky and deep chested, for their lungs had to adjust to the mountain air, his face was flat planed with Mongolian features, but down one side of his face, making his expression somehow more evil, more menacing, ran a puckered scar, livid against the copper skin. She guessed it had been made by a knife, and not long ago. The inevitable forage cap was pushed back on greasy curls which hung about his collar. He filled her with loathing and revulsion.

Now, as if he had tired of the subject of Manuel as a topic of conversation, he said abruptly, 'I am told you ask about the hostages.'

Suddenly Helen was very angry; all the pent up fear and anxiety came to boiling point as she was faced by this creature. The shock of finding Manuel associated with such scum, the kidnapping itself and the knowledge of what

Keith must be going through all came to a head.

'Don't you ennoble what you're doing — what you have done — by calling them hostages! They are victims, innocent victims of a bestial kidnapping and you know it!'

She knew her voice sounded shrill, uncontrolled, that she had lost her cool, but for the moment she didn't care. 'I am a doctor, I am concerned, as I have already told you. This whole place is filthy, unhygienic, some kind of infection could, if it started, sweep through here like wildfire. I wish to know where they are, what kind of condition they are in, for the sake of Humanity I demand — '

His fist crashed down on the packing case, splintering the wood, making Helen jump.

'I am Pablo — Pablo Gonzales — I am in command now.' He hissed the words at her like a snake, making her recoil once more. 'I am in command,' he repeated, as if to reassure himself as well as impress her, 'and no one *demands* of me — nothing is demanded here except by me.'

As suddenly as it had arisen, Helen's anger subsided. She realized it was as useless as banging her head against a brick wall. There was absolutely nothing she could do. She was helpless, completely in this man's power. Her only hope — and that a slim one — was to play along.

'In that case,' she said softly, 'I would have thought a man of your position would have realized it is in your own interest to keep your . . . ' she hesitated a moment, still reluctant to use the word, 'your hostages fit and well. Others in similar circumstances have found it paid off, I think.'

Now he turned the wick on the lamp up fully and for a few seconds sat looking at her, his eyes glittering, full of malevolence and hate. She wondered if she had gone too far — his hand slipped down on the holster of his gun . . . maybe this was it, perhaps he would simply shoot her out of hand where she stood . . .

Slowly he got up. Each moment seemed like an hour. He walked round the crate and came towards her, deliberately. Reaching out he took her face roughly in his hands. She closed her eyes against the horror, whatever it might be, the filthy, sickly-sour smell of him almost making her retch.

'A *beautiful* woman doctor,' he said softly, his warm, foetid breath on her cheek.

As suddenly as he had approached her he dropped his hands and turned away. Going to the door he opened it, barking out some instructions to a guard, which she couldn't understand. Then he turned back to her.

'As you are so anxious, you may have ten minutes with the Denholms . . . ten minutes and no more, those are my instructions.'

Once more the guard took her arm and pulled her roughly from the hut, pushing her in front of him across the compound, the men standing around watching curiously. Eventually she faced another closed door where two men with automatic rifles stood guard. They opened it and pushed her through with such violence that she fell to her knees on the floor of the hut. As she looked round she saw three startled pairs of eyes gazing at her from a pathetic little trio huddled on the edge of a bed much like the one Manuel lay on . . . the Denholms.

8

The hut was sparsely furnished, only slightly better than the one she had just left where Pablo sat like some evil spider in its web. At least here some of the windows still had an odd pane of glass left, the others had cardboard roughly nailed over them. There was a rickety table in the middle of the room which held some tin plates and mugs, upturned crates for chairs, a washstand with an enamel jug, a basin and bucket. Candles were stuck into bottles and a jar of what she supposed was drinking water, stood nearby.

Peggy looked grotesque against this background in her expensive Dior gown, her light sandals tossed on the ground. Even in the stale air Helen could still smell the expensive French perfume she had noticed she wore at the party. Now she was like a doll from whom all the sawdust had drained. All the vivacity had melted away, her face like a pale flower in the dim light, her eyes were enormous, and even from the middle of the hut, Helen could hear her breathing was laboured.

Nicholas had one arm in a makeshift sling, a filthy piece of khaki material obviously torn from an old uniform, his hair was matted with blood and dirt, and one eye half closed. She could see he had been pistol whipped as he let out an explosion of sound.

'Good grief, Helen, Helen Elliot!' He got to his feet and helped her up from her knees. For a moment his expression brightened. 'Have you come to tell us the ransom is paid, to release us. Did Keith send you?'

As he spoke, Mark, too, ran forward, his hands outstretched.

'I'm starving! I haven't had any breakfast. Have you brought us something to eat?'

The guard who stood inside the door, spat on the floor, making the child recoil, then the man shouted, 'Back, gringo,' waving his gun at Nicholas.

Helen shook her head. 'I'm afraid I'm only here in a kind of unofficial medical capacity.' She glanced round at the guerilla. 'One of their people got hurt.'

She bent over Peggy who seemed very distressed, her eyes swollen with crying, but somehow Helen was convinced her breathing difficulty was caused by more than tears and sobbing.

'Have you had trouble like this with your breathing before?' she asked gently, but before she could reply Nicholas broke in.

'Poor old sweetie, she gets like this at these god damned heights, the thin air. Can you help?'

'Not much unless I can get some oxygen.'

'I must say when I asked these swine for a medico for Peg, I never guessed it would be you, honey.' Nicholas' face was strained and Helen felt sure he had no illusions about the position they were in.

'Let me have a look at that arm,' she urged, 'then I'll do what I can for your wife.'

She unwound the filthy bandage and put on a dressing. At least it was clean.

'How did it happen?'

'I tried to hit the filthy pigs when they took hold of Peg. They hit me with their rifle butts . . . then they got me on the ground and kicked me . . . ' She nodded. 'But,' he went on, 'never mind about that. How the hell did you get here?'

As she worked she spoke softly. 'They brought me because my father had gone elsewhere, to another village, and I was alone at the clinic . . . but I had no idea where I was being taken. I would at least have put up some kind of resistance against them . . . '

He gave a lopsided grin which reminded her poignantly of Keith. 'Maybe that's our good luck then, but is someone of theirs wounded?'

'Yes, their leader, the man they call Il Paco, the Kid.'

'Good God!' Nicholas exploded. 'It sounds like something from a movie, an old Hollywood western.'

Helen put her finger to her lips, glancing round at the guard who was smoking a small cigar, his other hand still on his gun.

'The wound he has isn't bad. I have removed the bullet and cleaned it out. There isn't much danger of gangrene, but he has lost a lot of blood.' Now she turned back to Peggy, who grabbed both her hands.

'Please help me. It's this awful headache, and the nose bleed, that's the worst part.'

Helen delved into her medical bag and took out a roll of lint and some paper tissues.

'Let me mop you up a bit.'

'What are our chances?' Nicholas said in her ear as she bent over Peggy.

'Da Costa thought good. When I was at the police station with Keith this cassette came in from the guerillas. They were asking for food and clothes for the poor, to be financed by your company.'

'So . . . this is a political job is it, not personal?'

Helen shook her head. 'I don't honestly know. I think the only thing to do is play along, not aggravate them, and I do feel if this . . . ' she paused a moment, 'this man they call Il Paco — he seems to have a more lenient outlook than Pablo, or so it seemed at first when the cassette came in, but of course he has lost the leadership now — if he recovers and takes over, things perhaps may be better.' She felt she had said too much and prayed Nicholas wouldn't press her for an explanation.

'God give me patience,' was all he said, but Peggy, whom Helen had made lie down on the bed, raised herself on one elbow.

'That sounds good news at least, that they'd been in touch with Keith, maybe it'll only be a few hours . . . ' Her eyes were pleading that the others would agree. 'Will Keith know what to do, how to get the stuff?'

Nicholas looked away. 'I expect so, honey. He's a good boy.'

Peggy sank back on the greasy pillows, her whole body shaking. Helen brought a cologne spray from her handbag.

'Look, take this; it may help a bit, at least it's better than the smell of the blankets. I don't know if it's llama or goat. Can't be much to choose between them, I think.' She closed her bag. 'I'll try to arrange some fruit juice or milk for you, at the moment it might be better not to eat, specially the greasy kind of food they produce.'

'Don't worry, I can't swallow a thing; the very thought of it makes me throw up,' Peggy said. 'But it's Mark I'm worried about.' She glanced at the little boy where he sat now with Nicholas who had taken him over the other side of the hut. 'He's terribly highly strung. At the moment he's treating it all as a bit of a laugh, which Nick is trying to encourage, but he's so darn fussy over his food, and I guess I have spoilt him rotten . . . ' She closed her eyes and a couple of tears squeezed out between the lids.

Helen took her hand and pressed it. 'I shouldn't worry about that too much. Usually a small healthy boy will eat most things if he's hungry enough.'

And now, suddenly, as if his patience was exhausted, the guard came over and grabbed Helen once more with a flow of Spanish, and pushed her out of the door and into the compound, pulling her back to the hut where Manuel lay. As they moved across the dusty yard, a jeep came down the steep rutted road that led out of the camp. Flores was driving, but behind him, to her joy, she saw her father's old landrover. She pulled away from the guard and ran to him. Suddenly all the tension of the past few hours broke inside her and she threw herself into his arms. He looked utterly worn out in his crumpled, stained suit, dark with sweat and mud, an old knitted cap on his head, but he smiled and kissed her warmly, holding her close as the tears of relief ran down her face.

'Am I glad to see you,' she said as he released her at last and turned back to the landrover.

'I'll never forgive myself for being away when they came,' he said, his voice muffled as he drew some cardboard cartons from the rear of the vehicle. 'You wouldn't be in this godforsaken spot if I'd been there.'

She glanced round. Flores stood a little way off, his fingers drumming endlessly on the butt of his rifle, obviously having difficulty in concealing his impatience. She longed to question Steve about Manuel, to get some explanation but thought it better to wait until they were out of earshot of Flores.

'Did they tell you what I needed and did you manage to get it?'

'Some of it. I had to go down to the

hospital at Valdavero, that's why I've been so long. I had nothing at the clinic and had to talk the authorities into letting me have what I wanted. They were suspicious, of course, but fortunately I have always had the gift of the gab: Persuasiveness, I like to think.' He turned and gave her a broad grin as she took some of the packages from him.

'Let's go and look at this wound then,' he said, following Flores who had immediately walked swiftly towards the hut.

Juanita rose quickly as they entered. She had been sitting on one of the empty packing cases drawn up to the side of the bed.

'El Papa!' her eyes lit up. 'You will make him well, I know it.' She put her arms round Steve and kissed him.

'I shall try, I shall try, but as my daughter is as skilled as I, perhaps more so for she has had the modern training, I think no more could have been done had I been here.'

Juanita looked at Helen for a

moment as if she were sizing her up, then she turned. 'I will go to Pablo, tell him you are here. When I come back perhaps you will have good news.' She bent and kissed the unconscious Manuel and then went swiftly from the hut.

Steve was bending over Manuel, removing the dressings, and calling for the lamp. After a brief examination he straightened up.

'Excellent, you have done well, very well, particularly under such appalling conditions. Now we'll fix up the drip as best we can and get some blood back into him. He's young and healthy, he'll survive.'

Now she took his arm. 'Look, I must talk, you must explain. I just can't believe — couldn't believe — this is Manuel, I still can't believe it. I keep telling myself it isn't true, that it isn't him, it's some terrible nightmare. Surely there has been a mistake. The Manuel I knew could never get involved in such bestiality.' She was going to say more when the door was thrust open and Pablo swaggered into the hut. He held his rifle unslung in his hand. Steve swung round and seeing who it was, without speaking, nodded at him and indicated he should go back outside, following him swiftly before he had time to remonstrate. Helen felt more dazed and surprised than ever. It seemed her father knew all these people. He had left the door half open in his haste — she heard his voice raised in anger.

She went to the window and pulling aside the piece of sacking watched them where they stood a few yards away, Pablo stiffly with his hand inevitably on his gun, her father waving his arms around in a way she well remembered him doing when he was angry — and that was something which rarely happened, and was usually fully justified when it did.

At first she couldn't make head or tail of what they were both saying, then she heard Pablo shout, 'El gobierno mal

. . . the bad government . . . it is up to them . . . '

Her father banged his fist down on the bonnet of the landrover as he said, 'You know damned well Manuel asked for food, for clothing, for medicine, that is all. It was on the cassette, all that was wanted, needed, but you . . . you could not wait. All you want is money for yourself. You are no better than those you wish to rob — perhaps to murder . . . '

9

Her father's last words made Helen's blood run cold, it was as if the bottom of her world had fallen out. First of all the terrible shock of finding Manuel, her love, her childhood sweetheart, as the leader of this band of outlaws, for that is what they were to her — and now to realize her own father was involved. Her mind wouldn't accept — couldn't accept this knowledge.

At first when he returned to the hut, she was so bitterly angry and upset she couldn't speak. She pretended to be busy with the drips, trying desperately to get a grip on her feelings, to come to some kind of terms with this further ghastly situation. All her being rejected it as impossible.

Food was brought — everlasting soup, potatoes, what might have been either lamb or llama with rice; all of it tasted the same, of paraffin and grease. She tried to swallow some of the unsavoury mess. Whatever happened she must not become ill herself if she was to be of any use at all to the Denholms, and this now was what she pinned her faith on.

It seemed Steve was unaware of her change of mood.

'I shall have to return to the clinic,' he said, as he mopped up the gravy with the coarse black bread. It was as if he didn't notice what he ate either. She supposed for so long he had simply eaten to live and work, that it meant nothing to him.

She pushed her portion round on the chipped enamel plate, but at last she could contain herself no longer, the words burst from her in a furious torrent.

'You knew, didn't you, knew it was Manuel leading this gang, knew where he was, what he was doing, and yet you said nothing to Dona Maria and Carlos, lifelong friends who trusted you. How could you?'

He was lighting his pipe as she went on, the words falling over each other as if a dam had burst.

'I can't believe it, you and these ... these animals, that's all they are, they have no right to be called humans ... they don't know the meaning of the word humanity!'

He glanced at her now through the cloud of blue smoke, the fragrance of the tobacco reminding her sharply of her childhood ...

'Their leader is an old friend of yours, too. You must not be too ready to condemn, to judge until you have heard both sides.'

'Both sides!' The words exploded from her. 'There can be only one side to such behaviour, to kidnapping. It's little better than murder itself!'

Without answering, Steve got up and went over to the grate where the pitiful excuse for a fire smoked and spluttered, pushing at the wood with his foot in an unsuccessful attempt to produce some flame.

'To change the world one must first work with the world,' he said slowly. 'Don't you think it possible that Manuel has seen such misery, such poverty that being the kind of person he is he felt he had to do something about it? I'm no political animal, Nel. Nothing is further from my mind than the maze of politics. I have always thought most of the people from parish councillors to Prime Ministers were corrupt. I may be wrong, but I regret of course that you should disapprove — regret — but understand. What you must remember is this is not England. It is a different world, not just a different country. I am a healer doing my best. I have been here a lifetime, a lifetime of treating the poor, and I have seen the inequalities — '

'I know all that,' she broke in. 'I can see it, I have read of it, but it still cannot be an excuse for this kind of behaviour. What good can it possibly do? Violence breeds violence as da

Costa said . . . it is true.'

'It can also bring food and clothes to those who desperately need them, who will die without. That was Manuel's intention at least.' He paused a moment. 'Now I am not too sure, there are changes . . . Pablo . . . '

'Pablo!' She spat out the word. 'If he is in charge then there can be little hope for any of us.'

He shrugged and tamped the tobacco in the bowl of his pipe.

'I think . . . ' she had regained a little of her composure now after the relief of her outburst, 'I think that you and Manuel have forgotten people like Dona Maria and Carlos, and people like Pablo refuse to acknowledge they exist.'

'We haven't forgotten, Nel. You're wrong there, my dear. I know people think the peasants are self-sufficient, they say — the man has his llamas, they carry goods for him, he eats their flesh, burns their dung, his wife weaves clothes and sacks from the wool, they bring salt down from the mountains and return with grain, but they have no money at all. At night they simply stop and unload, the sacks shelter them from the wind and the llamas keep them warm while they sleep under the stars, but unless you have lived in an Indian village you cannot imagine the kind of lives they lead. Even if there is enough to eat, there is no comfort in their houses, they have nothing to distract their minds so they take to chicha and coca, their children suffer from a calcium deficiency so that their bones and teeth are often malformed. We have no right to stand in judgement, I think, only to help where we can.'

She got up. She had never heard Steve make such a long speech before, but there was nothing she could say in reply. 'I would like to leave as soon as I can.'

'And what about Manuel? He is your patient, what he has done should be of no consequence to you as a doctor.'

'I can do no more for him; you are

here now and it is you and your care they want.'

He hesitated a moment, then he took her hands and looked straight into her eyes.

'I think you must know it is impossible for you to leave — not only because of your patient, but because you know where the hostages are. You have virtually become one yourself.'

She snatched her hands away, turning from him, not trusting herself to speak.

He sighed. 'I must go. I shall try to return tomorrow, providing no one in the area has become suspicious. I shall have to be careful I am not followed.'

'Oh, yes,' she said sarcastically, 'playing along with Pablo — cops and robbers. It makes me ashamed to be your daughter.'

She did not see the pain in his eyes, and could not know that for a moment it was as if her mother had spoken . . .

She heard him drive away in the old landrover. She was alone now with

Manuel . . . she turned and looked at him. Flores called him Ortega, she knew, and so had Juanita. It had been his father's name, before he was adopted by the Cordobes. At least he had had the consideration to make sure there should be no possible connection with them and this Manuel who was the leader of a band of guerillas — at least he had had that amount of consideration, she thought bitterly.

She sat down on one of the crates, holding out her hands to the smoking wood which gave no warmth or comfort. She thought of all her father had said; it simply made her feel more desolate, more lonely, the feeling heightened now by the great wind which had risen and was whipping down the valley, bringing dust, she supposed from the distant parched fields.

She felt drained mentally and physically by all the horror of the last few hours. It seemed impossible that only a few days before she had been happy,

carefree, on board ship with Keith
. . . Keith . . . she hadn't had much
time to think about him, but now he
seemed like the only solid rock amidst
the swirling quicksand on which she
stood, this uncertain, horrific situation.
She wondered if she would ever see him
again. But for a moment, thinking of
him brought a little warmth. She
wrapped her arms about herself, closing
her eyes, trying to project herself back
to the few occasions on which he had
kissed her . . . then she remembered the
last time she had seen him, haggard,
drawn, as if he had aged ten years over
night. She longed to be able at least to
reassure him a little, to say, 'For the
moment at least they are still alive
. . . I'll do all I can, I promise . . . ' then
she came back again to the reality of
the present, the reality that indeed she
might never see him again, that she
might not be able to do anything for
Nick and Peggy and little Mark.

She got to her feet as desperation
flooded through her once more. There

was a slight sound behind her. She swung round. It had come from the bed. She went over. Manuel stirred.

She stood looking down at him, trying to remember how he had looked before, as a fifteen-year-old youth, strong, slim, golden with glowing health, her knight in shining armour . . . how that vision had tarnished! How could anyone change to such an extent, become someone quite unknown, alien, a different being?

For a moment she wondered if it could be true there was such a thing as being possessed by a devil as they had thought in olden days. Had some kind of evil spirit entered into these two men who had meant so much in her past — Steven and Manuel? It was a curious country, but they were the last two people she could possibly have imagined being involved in such barbarism.

She bent automatically to check the dressing on the wound. It was dry, the bleeding had stopped. She stood up and looked at the drip; it was nearly empty. Her father had pomised to come with more bottles of saline solution, more plasma, and oxygen for Peggy.

Slowly her gaze went back to Manuel's face. She caught her breath, startled as if she had been caught spying . . . his eyes were open; those dark, expressive, warm eyes that had reminded her of the big velvet pansies that grew in the garden at the hacienda . . .

Only now, although he was looking at her, and the eyes were the same she remembered — now they were cold, hard, like jet — there was no sign of recognition in them . . .

10

For a moment Helen felt a pang of disappointment that Manuel didn't recognize her — that, she knew, was allowing her heart to rule her head. The feeling was immediately followed by one of relief for she was reluctant he should know her true identity at the moment, her own emotions were in such a turmoil; first that Steve himself was so deeply implicated with the kidnappers — and secondly the fact that as a woman she was still drawn to Manuel, not only as a doctor to patient, but because she could not forget the past. But it was still impossible for her to find any reason to forgive or condone his behaviour. On the other hand she had to admit he hadn't had a chance to state his case. She knew, too, that her patient, in spite of the slight improvement was still very weak, although given some luck, added to her medical knowledge and the meagre equipment available, at least he would not die. He still had a high fever, which accounted partly for the fact that he had not recognized her, of that she was sure. Under normal circumstances, in spite of the long time since they had met, surely he would have recognized someone who had been so close, someone she had once believed and hoped that he loved.

She turned away, satisfied for the moment with his condition, her thoughts now turning to the Denholms with whom her feelings and concern rested in the main, and to Keith himself, hundreds of miles away in Valdavero, who she knew must be suffering the agony of the damned wondering what was happening. But perhaps most of all she felt a deep concern over Pablo for it was obvious from his behaviour, his arrogance and assertiveness, that he was getting more and more power over the guerillas and encouraging them to talk of money, a ransom for these valuable hostages, not just clothes and food . . .

Helen had been sleeping on a makeshift bed in the same hut as Manuel so she could be on hand if he needed anything, but now she was told by Juanita that it would be 'more convenient' if she were moved elsewhere. She had already learned there was not much point in arguing with either Juanita or Pablo — and Manuel was in no condition to be appealed to.

The hut she was given was only a few yards from his. As with the others, it contained simply an iron bed with two blankets, a table with a jug and basin, a small paraffin stove for heat and an oil lamp for light.

Flores took her across the compound with an apology as he opened the door.

'It is poor, Señora, but no worse than the rest of us have.' He gave a rueful grin. She hadn't seen much of him since they had arrived at the camp, apart from the first couple of days, although once or twice he had put his head round the door to ask how Manuel was. He and Pablo spoke little, and when Juanita appeared he turned his eyes away as if he did not wish to acknowledge her existence. In a way his attitude brought Helen a certain amount of comfort; it seemed he was not like the rest of the guerillas, or Pablo himself, and she wondered why he had not been chosen as second in command. She noticed, too, that it was always he who was sent to fetch Steven when he was needed urgently.

Her father had said he would be back as soon as possible with more oxygen for Peggy, and further medical supplies. Now the hours seemed to drag by on leaden feet. She whiled away some of the time by making as appetizing meals as she could for the Denholms. She supposed the guerillas themselves had some kind of communal canteen or cookhouse for she never saw any of them in the one she used, and Flores brought her stores from somewhere else when she asked for them — such as they were. Mostly tinned or dehydrated food, the diet was monotonous, with no fresh fruit or vegetables. Also she was anxious about Peggy who was still very poorly; in fact at one time she had thought of asking Flores to go and fetch Steven for the woman hardly ate anything, but spent most of her time sleeping, and she had become pale and drawn, the bones showing through the taut skin of her face. She realized it was useless to ask Pablo or Juanita for help. What was being done about the arrangements for the drop she didn't know; she supposed they were waiting now until Manuel was well enough to be consulted, and then the emissaries would be chosen.

She had just crawled into the filthy blankets, trying not to think of the germs and other horrors they held, when she heard a couple of rifle shots, a shout and then swift footsteps coming towards the hut. It was impossible for her to lock the door on the inside and the fastenings were rusty. She sat up in bed, drawing her duffle coat around her, expecting it would be Pablo who would erupt into the hut — but there was a knock — insistent, urgent . . .

'Come in,' she called, 'it isn't locked.'

Flores stood in the doorway, a lamp swinging in his hand, the light shining on his red beard. It reminded her of the first time she had seen him.

'Señora, please to come quickly. It is Mr Denholm. He ask me to fetch you. He tried to come himself, but there was shooting, he is not allowed from the hut.'

Helen jumped out of bed, pulling on the coat, and slipping her bare feet into her shoes.

'Is Mr Denholm badly hurt?'

Flores shook his head. 'No, Señora Doctor, he is not hurt, the bullets, they miss. It is not he that I come for, it is the Señora Denholm; she is sick, very sick with the breathing. Please to come as soon as you can.'

Her heart sank as she followed Flores

across the compound, dark and still under the moonless sky, only the guards on the door of the Denholms' hut still stood with their rifles at the ready. The door was ajar and Helen could hear Mark crying and Nicholas' voice as he tried to soothe him. Swiftly she went over to the bed where Peggy lay, her mouth open as she drew in painful, shuddering breaths. It was pitiful to watch as she struggled for air.

'Thank God you've come. She's been like this for hours, but these swine wouldn't let me call you. That pig Pablo — I asked for you ages ago, but he said it is only the mountain sickness and all gringos have it, it will go.'

Helen nodded and turned to Flores. 'Please fetch me the small oxygen mask from Manuel's hut.'

She listened to Peggy's chest; her pulse was rapid and she had a fever, but there was no congestion of the lungs as she had at first feared. She turned back to Nicholas.

'As a matter of fact Pablo is right,'

she grinned. 'Although I hate to have to admit it, it is simply the soroche, but she needs a little help with her breathing. We must keep her warm and I'll give you some pills for her — antibiotics — they'll help a little.' She went to her bag and shook out some pills, passing them to Nicholas, who grabbed her arm.

'Look I want the truth — how ill is she? If it's bad I'll kill that swine with my own hands, I swear it!'

Helen tried to smile, to reassure. 'Honestly, it isn't dangerous, just very uncomfortable and a bit frightening.' She'd never seen anyone look more grim than Nicholas. She dreaded to think what he would do if anything did happen to Peg.

Flores returned with the oxygen and she fixed the mask over Peg's mouth; gradually her breathing eased and she smiled at Helen as she lifted it off for a moment. 'Thanks. I've never had it this bad before, maybe it's partly nerves.'

Helen nodded. 'More than likely. Just

try to relax. I'll leave this with you. Don't use it for too long at a time, just when you feel you can't take any more.'

A storm had broken suddenly with lashing rain and wind as Flores took her back to her own hut. Wearily she struggled behind him through its fury across the muddy compound, longing for a bath, a change of clothes, a clean bed to sleep in. She had had enough of South America — more than enough. Somehow, if they ever got out of this situation, she would persuade Steve to return to England with her. But if he still stubbornly refused, then she would return without him. She did not want to remain in the country longer than she had to, but even as these thoughts went through her mind, the idea of Manuel — Manuel as he used to be, came also to her, as she had remembered him down the years, always hoping one day to see him again. If he still survived, if he still proved to be the old Manuel of childhood, could she leave him now? And then what about

Juanita? How deeply involved was he with her?

Flores closed the door behind him and she sank down on the bed. A thrill of warm desire as she thought of Manuel suddenly overwhelmed her, so powerful she felt quite dizzy, remembering the curve of his mouth as he smiled, the way his eyes would light up, his face puckish with laughter, and the gentle way he had with an animal or bird that was sick or injured. That was surely the real Manuel if she could peel back the layers that had obscured that character.

She got up and leaned against the door to close it; it had blown open again in the wind. She was so tired now she could hardly make the effort to peel off her sodden clothes. Earlier she had rinsed out her pyjamas in some of the brackish water and dried them over the stove; they smelt of paraffin and smoke, but it was the best she could do. She wrapped her sodden hair in a towel and consoled herself with the thought of the doctors who had had to carry on their work under war conditions, conditions far worse than these.

Although it was past midnight the camp still seemed to have some life and movement about it. Somewhere a man laughed, another shouted, voices were raised in an instant quarrel to be hushed again as quickly. There was the sound of a guitar, and then an oddly soothing voice somewhere singing a Spanish love song; for some strange reason it evoked a warm summer evening in a world far away . . .

She wished she could lock the door on the inside. In spite of Steve's assurances about her being safe, she felt nervous, a growing apprehension, the howl of the wind adding to the feeling as it buffeted the flimsy hut. The rain must have ceased as she could no longer hear it drumming on the tin roof of the hut. From sheer exhaustion she collapsed on the bed and almost immediately forgot everything in sleep.

But now her dreams were filled with terror. The kind of dream where one is chased by something horrific and becomes completely paralysed. Something was closing in on her. In vain she tried to beat it off. She was being suffocated. A hand over her mouth . . . hot breath on her cheek . . . She struggled, tried to scream and woke up, slow to re-orientate from dream to reality.

It was no dream, no nightmare. Someone — a dark shadow — stood in the dimness of the hut, there was a hand over her mouth. She was conscious that the storm had blown itself out, the whole world was quite still.

A voice said softly, 'Do not be frightened, it is I, Pablo.' She had never heard him speak like that before, and for some reason the very gentle tone of his voice was far more menacing than when he shouted in his usual manner. In her heart she was convinced he was capable of anything including rape and murder. She tried to speak, to struggle up in the bed, but he held her in a vice-like grip.

'That is better, although I do not like to take my women too easily, a little struggle adds to the — how you say — the conquest — is delightful, but not too much, I think, eh?'

She could feel his breath on her lips as his mouth pressed down on hers. He stank of drink and tobacco and rotten teeth. She tried to turn her head away, her lips bruised and bleeding, his free hand pulled down the blankets.

'Do not struggle, Mi amor. I am sure you would give freely without such fight to our friend Manuel, if he asked, si? I have watched the desire in your eyes.'

He ripped the front of her pyjamas and at last she managed to pull her head up and opening her mouth, dug her teeth with all her strength into his thumb.

For a moment the pain did not register on his nerves, then he let out a howl of pain and a torrent of expletives. What might have happened next she did not dare to think as the door was flung open, the light from a lantern filled the hut and a woman's voice shrieked Pablo's name, followed by a similar flow of invective. He swung round to see Juanita standing with her hands on her lips, glaring like a tigress, behind her, Flores with the lamp, its light shining on the faces of some of the other guerillas in the open doorway.

'So, you find favour now with the gringo doctor?' Juanita spat at him.

He grinned at her, trying at the same time to suck the wound Helen had inflicted on his thumb.

'You know it is not so, mi amor. I came to see the door was properly fastened for I do not trust her, and as I tried the lock she pulled it open and invited me inside. I thought it was some matter she wished to discuss about Il Paco, but she . . . ' He broke off as if in modesty, dropping his gaze, and Helen found it difficult to believe Juanita could be taken in by such blatant deceit. 'She tried to make love to me . . . I did not realize . . . I thought it might be medical supplies she wanted . . .'

Behind Pablo, Flores had moved slightly. Helen glanced at him. In the lamplight she could see the expression on his face, his fear of Pablo, struggling with something else — perhaps a longing to protect her which he dared not put into action.

The other men crowded in the doorway, seeming to hold their breath, waiting, hoping for some excitement, violence perhaps. How would these two men, both so different, react now?

But it was Juanita who made the next move, her fury centred on Helen as the latter tried to pull the clothes back over her shivering body.

'So, under the pretence of being a gringo doctor you are trying to take my man, is that it?'

Before Helen could make any reply the girl had gone on, 'You English are pigs.' She spat on the blanket. 'You pretend to be so pure, but you have no morals, nothing.'

She turned on her heel. Pablo

meanwhile had regained most of his equilibrium, and turned to Flores.

'You can go, Cobulla, and take these others with you. It is quite simple for me to handle the situation. If I need you, I will call.'

Juanita walked away from the bed as if Helen no longer interested her, and taking Pablo's arm said, 'Come, compadre, these people we do not need.'

The significance of the name Pablo had called Flores did not escape Helen — Cobulla, the horse . . . Flores was undoubtedly one of the strongest of the men in the camp physically, but she knew from his attitude that Pablo looked upon him only as an ignorant peasant — she knew, too, it was obvious he had no love or care for the peasants, but although Flores might not be too bright, Pablo also had the sense to know he was loyal to the cause, a man he could not afford altogether to antagonize . . . it seemed, too, that Juanita had changed her allegiance — had that some significance?

As she lay shivering in the hard narrow bed, she realized only too well that she and the Denholms were sitting on a powder keg . . .

11

The next morning Helen was attempting to prepare some kind of stew for the Denholms, the best she could do under the circumstances, and it was the sound of it boiling over on the stove that brought her back to reality. Inside she was still trembling from the events of the previous night. But now remembering the immediate task in hand, she filled the tin plates with the savoury mess, wrinkling up her nose. It didn't really smell too bad.

Peggy looked a little better now. Some colour had returned to her cheeks and she was breathing without the portable oxygen cylinder. Helen helped her to sit up against the hard pillow and put the plate in front of her. Involuntarily she retched at the sight and smell.

Helen grinned. 'Honestly, it isn't too

bad. I made it myself and at least I can assure you it is clean and wholesome, if unappetizing. Try to eat a little.'

Peggy gave a weak attempt at a smile. 'I'm sorry, I didn't mean to appear ungrateful. You're so kind, I don't know what we would have done without you.' She took Helen's hand in hers for a moment. 'You didn't have much time with Keith, but I hope . . . ' she paused for a minute, 'I was going to say 'when' we get back to civilization, perhaps I'd better alter it to 'if' — then I hope we shall see much more of you, my dear.'

Helen smiled back. She had no intention of repeating what had occurred with Pablo, it was obvious they didn't realize that the whole situation had undergone a subtle change. She would have to talk to Steve, see if he could get some sense into Manuel as soon as he was better. Surely the idea of hostages, of money and all that entailed, could only be a temporary idea thought up by Pablo — of course, at the moment Manuel was totally unaware of what was going on.

Mark and Nicholas accepted the stew with alacrity. The little boy was so hungry he declared he could eat a horse.

'Honest, if you had one I sure could.'

Nicholas squeezed her hand. 'Thanks for what you've done for Peg, any news of when we may expect to get out of this hell hole?'

She shook her head, not daring to meet his eyes lest he should read the feeling of apprehension she knew must show in them. 'I'll bring you some coffee in a minute. The cooking arrangements are rather primitive, and I can really only manage to heat one thing at a time. The only bright spot is they do let me move from my hut to yours without protest, if under strict guard.'

He covered her hand with his. 'I'll come and fetch it, there's no reason why you should wait on us.' He went towards the door and opened it. As he did so a rifle barrel was thrust into his chest by one of the guards.

'Back, gringo. No one is allowed out of the hut but the Señora doctor.'

Helen could see the mounting fury on Nicholas' face and quickly stepped in front of him.

'It's all right, Señor Denholm was only going to carry a tray of coffee for me.'

'It is command from Señor Gonzalez; no one crosses the compound without his permission.'

'Who in hell is Gonzalez?' Nicholas shouted.

Gently Helen took his arm and pulled him back inside the hut, her finger to her lips. 'It's Pablo — Pablo Gonzalez.'

'Is it, by heck, and who does he think he is, giving us orders? I thought this chap Manuel or Ortega, whatever his name is, was in charge of this rabble.'

Helen prayed the guard didn't understand the last word and its meaning.

'He is, but at the moment he is too ill to take charge. Pablo is his second in command.'

She knew her voice had faltered as she mentioned Pablo's name. Nicholas gave her a swift glance.

'Something's very wrong, isn't it?' He shook her gently by the shoulder. 'Best tell me what it is, honey.'

She was about to assure him that until she had talked to Steve there was nothing she could tell him, when Mark came running over and saved her for the moment. Having finished his stew he demanded, 'What's for pudding?'

She bent down and whispered in his ear as if it were a great secret between them, 'Tinned guavas.'

He wrinkled his nose. 'No ice cream?'

'I'm afraid not, but I'll see if there's some tinned milk.'

She crossed the compound, the guard trailing along behind her with his rifle slung on his shoulder. She piled the tray with enamel jugs of coffee, and the tin of fruit. They would have to help themselves on the same plates from which they had eaten their stew. Most of the niceties of the kind of civilization they were used to were totally lacking, but even so they wouldn't starve. She pulled herself up short; already she had herself become absorbed into thinking in the terms of some kind of 'them' and 'us' situation. Was it as contagious as that?

Flores came to the door of the hut.

'You are wanted, Señora Doctor, in Il Paco's hut. Your father is there,' he dropped his glance, 'and also Pablo.'

'Manuel is no worse?' she asked quickly as she followed him from the hut.

He shook his head. 'No, he is conscious. It is some kind of talk or discussion, I think.'

Pablo stood with his hands on his hips, a sneer on his lips. It was obvious he had been quarrelling with Manuel who was half propped up, half lying in the bed, his face pale and drawn. She was about to protest that he was in no fit state for any discussion nor for talk even, but she caught Steve's eye as he gave a faint shake of his head. He, too, looked worn out, and he felt it for he was upset that Helen despised what he had done. He had tried to explain how he felt — he certainly was not entirely contrite; his reasons for his association with the guerillas had been a genuine concern for the people whom he knew so well — but now it seemed things had got out of hand and he was deeply worried.

Pablo glanced at Helen, defiance on his face as if he dared her to repeat what had happened last night. You needn't worry, she thought, I'll keep it till the time is right.

'So, the female gringo is sick?' he said sarcastically. 'It is no wonder for they live the soft life and cannot even stand the climate in which so many of our people have to exist.'

'I should doubt if it has anything to do with the señora's life style; she obviously has a weak chest and the shock has not helped,' Helen said coldly.

'It is certainly not the result of malnutrition,' Pablo said scornfully.

'I think it matters little what has brought it on; the fact remains the longer she stays up at this altitude, the worse she will get.'

Pablo turned away as though he had lost interest and addressed his remarks to Steve and Manuel.

The heat in the hut was oppressive. Helen sat down on one of the crates longing for a cool drink that wasn't just brackish warm water. None of the three men looked at her, she might have been part of a backcloth.

'We have three members of the gringo family,' Pablo said abruptly, 'and we are going to demand cash for them, an adequate sum for such people. I have decided this will be five million American dollars.'

There was complete silence — sounds from outside came faintly to the hut, an engine revved up, a snatch of song. For some reason Helen's mind strayed to other kidnapping cases she had read, and the victims' fates . . .

Manuel had drawn himself up in the bed and now he said softly, 'That is not possible, amigo . . . '

Pablo shrugged impatiently. 'I think it is not only possible, it is necessary.' His voice, too, was low, but in his case with cunning, as he went on, 'The money will provide more food than the other way; it can be spread over a wider area, and I know what is required by my people better than any gringo does.'

Steve turned to look at Manuel, but he said nothing.

'The men are discontented with the present situation,' Pablo went on, 'impatient, naturally they want things to move along. Also there is always the danger we may be attacked by army patrols which rove the district, apart from the police.'

He paused a moment, then went on, 'I am planning to send the gringo

Nicholas Denholm to organize the money with his son — this Keith has done nothing, nothing at all. Then once the money is secure, certain, the female gringo can be released, not until. The boy is to remain until the getaway is complete.'

Steve shifted his weight from one foot to the other and said, 'I have a much better idea, Pablo — but of course it is only a suggestion; you are the one to decide.'

For a moment Pablo had looked annoyed at the interruption, but as the last part of the sentence sunk into his mind his expression softened a little. He had nothing against the doctor — yet.

'Do you not think perhaps it would be better to return Mrs Denholm first, as she is sick and something of a liability? Also, being a woman, she will be able to be more persuasive with her own son, specially as her husband and younger child are still hostages.'

Pablo scowled. 'I think that is too

much to ask. Even our own leader, Il Paco — even he could not be taken to hospital for treatment. Why should the female gringo be released merely because she has a little trouble with her breathing?'

Helen made an impatient gesture and opened her mouth to speak, but her father frowned at her behind Pablo's back.

It was obvious now that Pablo was uncertain of his ground as he turned over Steve's words in his mind.

'Is the female gringo to be trusted? Women seldom are.'

Steve said slowly, 'I'm prepared to vouch for the Señora.'

Pablo gave him a long cool look and then said, 'Very well, no one will be able to say I am not humane, that I do not listen to reason, but there will be conditions . . . '

For a moment Helen was so relieved at his decision she didn't worry what the conditions might be, but then with mounting dismay she heard him say,

'The money then is to be brought to an old chapel on the lower slopes of the mountains, one that is not used today.' He paused a moment and then turned towards Manuel as if to make sure he would receive the full impact of his words. 'The money is to be brought there by Don Carlos de Cordobes.'

Helen glanced at her father. His face was expressionless.

'It won't be easy, any of it,' he said, 'specially contacting Don Carlos.'

'It will be arranged,' Pablo said shortly, 'but I must warn you all that if anything goes wrong through careless-ness on your part, then we send a message to the gringo Keith to tell him Señora Helen will be shot as proof of our intentions.'

Without saying any more he turned on his heel and left the hut. Steve went over to where Helen sat, trembling, trying to still the shaking of her limbs. He put his arm round her.

'Look, we have no alternative. I suppose it seems to Pablo this use of

Don Carlos in some way bridges the gap between the 'them' and 'us' situation, although I doubt if those are the words he would use — between the money owning Americans and the peasants . . . he knows now, too, that Don Carlos will find out that Manuel is involved in the kidnap and this will ensure he doesn't go to the police. It is an ironic situation, the choice of Manuel's adopted father and all he stands for — the man is no fool.'

Nicholas himself was torn between relief that Peggy was to be released from the camp and fear at what might happen to her between the hideout and safety in Valdavero.

Peggy herself was close to hysteria at the thought of leaving Mark and Nicholas.

'There is no other way, my dear,' Steve had said gently. He and Helen made her as comfortable as they could in the back of the vehicle, laying an old mattress on the floor. Pablo insisted that she be blindfolded until well away from the camp. Two young guerillas were to go as well, one to drive, one to sit in the back with Peggy. She had been given clear written instructions which she was to take directly to Don Carlos, and it had been made very definite that if she contacted anyone at all before the drop was completed, Nicholas and Mark would be shot . . . Steve was to go with them, which brought a small measure of comfort to Nicholas as he watched them go, murmuring, 'Adios, my darling. I'll get even with the bastards one day.' Mark clung to his trouser leg, white and speechless, Helen stood holding his other hand in hers. She crouched down and wiped his tear-streaked face.

'You'll soon see mummy again, and she'll be much better with that nasty old chest trouble all gone.'

They stood, a pathetic little group, until the dust cloud behind the jeep had settled, then Nicholas and Mark went back into the hut where Flores had put a tray of coffee and orange juice. Helen had been told by Pablo to return to Manuel's hut. At the door, Nicholas turned to her.

'What chance has she, Helen — what chance have any of us? I'd like the truth.'

Helen said slowly. 'The truth — I often wonder just what the word means, everyone seems to interpret it differently — but Peggy will improve as soon as she gets to a lower latitude. The soroche is very debilitating. Good food and rest will help, and at least she couldn't be in better hands than my father's.'

She turned away and followed Pablo into Manuel's hut. Her mind was buzzing with thoughts, with questions — suppose Don Carlos refused to come because of leaving Dona Maria — and what effect would the whole thing have on Maria herself, for now she would have to be told exactly how Manuel was involved, and already she was far from well. She remembered how the old lady had said, 'Not to know is terrible, even perhaps to know he was dead would be better.' So perhaps even to know her beloved 'son' was a kidnapper would be better than nothing. Now she wished she could see Tante Maria herself and explain, for she was beginning at last to understand some of the questions which had puzzled her.

At the door of the hut Pablo said derisively, 'So, let us hope that your father and the female gringo between them do not make a mess of this situation, which is usually the way of the British and Americans.'

Before she could reply he had gone.

She went slowly into the hut. Manuel was still propped up against the greasy pillows, his eyes reflecting the setting sun.

She knew he must have heard Pablo's remarks and wondered what he made of them. She wasn't left long in doubt for he held out his hand and in the voice she remembered from childhood, murmured the name which he had always used for her —

'Elena!'

12

'Elena!' The sound of the half-forgotten name he had used for her in their childhood days startled her, taking her winging back for a moment into the past, but she spoke, before she had time to think.

'Yes — what is it?' she asked.

'Little Elena, the beautiful, cool Elena . . . is it possible? I must really be dreaming.'

'Not only possible but true.' She turned away now, not able to bear the look in his eyes. 'I had come to South America . . . ' she paused, 'as you must know, my father hasn't been well, is desperately overworked . . . I had to come to try to persuade him to return to England with me — and I got involved in all this.' She waved her hand round the hut. 'Naturally, I had been looking forward to seeing Dona Maria,

Don Carlos — and you — again, to talking about the old days, but I hardly imagined it would be like this.'

'Like what?' There was a little edge to his voice.

She turned and faced him. 'As an outlaw, a guerilla, a terrorist, a rebel — or whatever name you like to give yourself.' The pent up words burst out from her now.

The edge on his voice had turned to anger.

'They are the names others give us — who says what is true?' For a moment it was as if her own words had been turned in on her, then he went on, 'Your view is from one side of the wall, mine from the other.'

Fighting down the retort which rose to her lips, she said with a professional calm she certainly did not feel, 'You must rest. Later we will talk.'

'Oh no, I have much to say to someone like you, your father's daughter. I had of course heard you were a doctor, too. It is important you listen, please, Elena . . . '

Realizing he would not rest until he had talked she drew up a packing case, then tried to arrange his pillows to give him the most support possible.

'At least lie back and try to relax. You have lost a lot of blood. You need rest — and good food.'

'It was while I was at college,' he said, as if he had not heard. 'It had nothing to do with politics, it was a student federation. All we wanted for our country was freedom — freedom to write, to speak, to think. For some reason I seemed to be the one who took on more and more responsibility. I realize now to some extent I showed a foolish opposition to any form of control. The secret police began to purge all the universities of what they called subversives, dissidents, and so before the course ended I had to leave or I would have been expelled in any case. That I could not do to Tante Maria and Don Carlos.' He paused.

Helen got up and fetched some fruit

juice which Flores had brought in earlier. 'So you came back to Boldivia secretly, I suppose.'

'Yes, I had no hope of resuming my studies.' He looked directly at her now. 'At one time I had thought of becoming a doctor like El Papa. I think I admire him more than any other human being I have ever met.'

'Go on,' she said, as he hesitated.

'I managed to cross the border, with the help of Juanita.' He dropped his gaze from her candid eyes. 'Her father is rich, a land owner in Peru, but she despises his wealth, feels as I do. She had an allowance left to her by her mother which he cannot touch; this we lived on for a time, roaming like nomads, living in caves, doing casual labour, anything, until gradually we built up a small nucleus who felt the same way.'

'Against law and order.' She could not keep the bitterness out of her voice.

'No,' he said quietly, his face drawn now so that she put out her hand to restrain him from further talk, leaving her fingers briefly on his lips. He took her hand in his. 'Dear Elena, it is wonderful to see you again — but no, you are not right. We found that freedom to speak is not everything; the trouble with our country is the terrible inequalities, that is what we must end.'

She got up quickly. 'I've heard it all before somewhere — a hundred times.'

'Perhaps. But to each who suffers it is fresh.'

Now she stood looking at him, the memories flooding back. And for some reason, remembering their childhood, she realized that in a way they were still two of a kind, for she, too, was an idealist, people should be allowed to have the same equal opportunities. She supposed basically they were in tune — but somewhere they had grown apart. She knew, too, she was still deeply attracted to him — whether she was in love was impossible to analyse, but she did realize that all the years between had in a way been coloured by her love for him — she was a woman first — and she knew that whatever people might say to the contrary, in the ultimate where a man they loved was concerned, women's hearts ruled their heads. Manuel had been her own first sweetheart, her first love and as the Bible said — where your treasure is there will your heart be also.

'We thought those golden days of childhood would last forever,' she said softly. 'Swimming in the pool, boating on the lake where you taught me to fish — do you remember that time I cast a fly and caught a swallow on the wing?' The line had screamed through the reel as the poor thing struggled to be free, and with gentle hands he had removed the barbed hook and released it so it flew towards the sun and as they shaded their eyes she had said, 'Free — to be free — that is what we all want.' Now the words came winging back to her lips like the bird itself, and she thought how many people had left one kind of bondage for what they had thought was freedom, only to find it was another prison of a different kind. He looked at her now with shadowed eyes.

'It's no good talking to people about freedom when all they want or need is survival. I realize that now. I realize, too, that things have gone badly wrong, Elena, but you must believe that I have faith, belief in what I am trying to do — even if the approach may seem wrong to you.'

She turned away for she knew very well what he had been reading, whose works he had studied, she had seen some of the guerillas even with copies of Lenin and Marx in their hands. In spite of all that she had felt they were on a different wavelength; it was as if in reality they could not communicate at all.

'You have to remember life in a country like this is marginal, entirely dependent on seasons, so if summer rains fail the effect can be a disaster, the potato crop fails, pastures are destroyed

— many are so concerned with only private profit, and so few with public good . . . '

All this she had glimpsed only as a child, all this her mother had tried to tell her, Helen now realized. She knew that people like Don Carlos were few and far between, and that now Manuel really believed he was fighting for a kind of revenge on whoever was keeping down the ordinary people. For a moment she thought perhaps she did see a pattern — then she remembered Nicholas, Peggy and little Mark. Were they innocent or guilty? Who could judge? Who could tell? Wearily she pushed the hair back from her face; it all seemed such a muddle, so hopeless. She remembered her father's words, so often repeated, 'to change the world one must first work with the world.' It was something she had really never understood, now perhaps she was starting to.

Once more she took his hand, still hot with fever, but she had to know.

'What really happened? What made you into this kind of person, made you forget Dona Maria and Don Carlos and all the old times?'

He didn't answer for a moment, then he said softly, 'I haven't forgotten, but unless you have lived among the Indians you can't imagine what their lives are like. It is no wonder they have taken to chicha and coca.' She remembered what her father had said on the same subject.

'That worries me — the drug.'

He shrugged. 'It is not really habit forming. I don't think it does much harm; they seem able to kick the habit if they wish, and it makes a man able to bear cold, hunger, exhaustion and despair.'

'I shall never see any justification for encouraging men to take drugs, not under any circumstances,' she said forcibly.

'Then you should not justify giving a man an anaesthetic to relieve a different kind of pain, and yet you as a doctor do so. Perhaps we cannot tell the point when something that has been given by God for man's benefit ceases to be good and becomes evil, perhaps even we should leave such decisions to God himself.'

At least, she thought, some of Dona Maria's teaching has remained with him.

'We felt, as students, we couldn't trust anyone. The Government seemed just to want a few good quality brains from amongst us, a kind of cream of intelligentsia; the rest they considered peasants, beneath contempt.'

'Wouldn't it have been better just to get on with your studies and leave politics to people who understand them?' she said.

'Perhaps then we would be too old . . .'

She swung round from the medical case she had been tidying as he spoke. 'As a humanitarian I have to agree with much of what you say, but to take it out on a woman and small child by kidnapping — in this I can see no reason.'

He shifted a little uneasily in the bed. 'I, too, loathe violence. Originally I had suggested an alternative — that we kidnap only Keith Denholm for ransom in kind, clothes and food, but . . . ' he hesitated.

'I know,' she said slowly, 'you were overruled — the little revolutionaries must have their day.'

She stood looking down into his eyes seeing herself reflected in miniature in their dark depths. Suddenly, woman-like, she longed to ask about Juanita, to say — 'Do you still love me?' knowing it was a kind of madness in her own blood. She thought of the years she had spent in study, the dedication she felt for her profession, her determination that whatever might offer in the way of a job, she would stay true to the resolve to help the sick always no matter what their politics, colour or creed. Healing was the priority, the yardstick, and she felt sure in his own way Manuel had the same tenets — the need to help the weak, the underdog.

Then she thought of Pablo, of Juanita. They had probably seen how easily others got money without effort, without pity or compassion.

'You spoke of the little revolutionaries,' he said, as if reading her mind. 'That above all is what I want to avoid — up in the sierra land-hungry peasants starve and die of malnutrition — sometimes there are raids between ranches, the burning of barns, stealing livestock — in some places they are forming secret syndicates — it is a warning, it could lead to a bloodbath. You must believe that.'

Suddenly he grinned, as if to relieve the tension they had built up between them.

'This is not your peaceful England,' he said. 'You have to remember that, Elena . . . '

Now the hours and days seemed to drag more than they had before even. Helen knew she trod a knife edge where

Pablo was concerned. She knew the price of any slips would be not only the death of herself, but of Nicholas and Mark, too; she had no illusions on that point.

At first she had found it difficult to accept, as if she were poised on the brink of an abyss into which she might plunge at any moment — Death. She had encountered it many times in her career — in other people — but had never seriously applied the possibility to herself.

She asked Manuel what she had done to incur Pablo's hate.

'You don't have to do anything, it's what you *haven't* done. In the eyes of him and the rest you are condemned — you and all the gringos with whom they connect you.'

'And for that we should pay with life?'

'So they think.'

'But you don't, not you Manuel.' It was as near to an entreaty as she could bring herself.

He shook his head. 'No, and that I suppose is where the dividing line comes, the difference, and for that Pablo and Juanita will not forgive you or me.'

Her anxiety had been for Don Carlos, too, with this new plan. 'What is the procedure?'

Again he shrugged. 'As you know, Nicholas is to be taken to the rendezvous, Mark remains here with us — when they have the money and are safely away,' he dropped his gaze, 'then the intention, as it was put to me, is that you will be returned to safety.'

'And you?' she asked softly.

'That I cannot tell. On the surface it is assumed, I suppose, that when I am fit I shall resume leadership, provided I am willing to conform with their ideas.'

'If you don't . . . if you can't after this . . . '

He closed his eyes and lay back wearily on the pillow.

'That I do not know, but much of course depends on Don Carlos.'

She got up and went across to the dirty window, wiping some of the dust from it and gazing out at the barren waste, the compound where one or two guerillas paced up and down, or leant against a vehicle smoking . . . of Pablo and Juanita there was no sign.

'If only we knew what was happening down there in Valdavero,' she said slowly.

13

Often Steve drove like a madman. He always seemed to have to be in a hurry; there were always too few hours in the day, too few days in the week, but now with Peggy sick he tried to keep the landrover as much on an even keel as he could, but it still lurched and swayed from pothole to pothole. The young guerilla who had been driving when they left the camp, was quite content to let Steve take over, knowing he was more used to driving in the terrain — the man himself usually went on foot or the back of a mule. In places the road was a mere track with no more than two iron hard ruts through thick scrub, in others it was worn smooth and barely visible across the naked bedrock. He wrested with the kicking twisting steering wheel in concentrated silence, staying on the road by nothing more than brute strength and lightning-fast reactions.

They drove through the night and just after dawn the track along which they bounced and jarred had the surface of a washboard, but they were approaching the last lap and this lifted his spirits a little.

The guerilla who sat beside him spoke little. He hugged his gun to him as if his life depended on it. He knew, of course, that Steve was not armed; at least that he did not carry a gun on his person, although he had an old service revolver in the cubby hole of the vehicle. Really he had no idea why for it was most unlikely he would ever have used it.

Now and then the young man, who had told him his name was Miguel, drank from a bottle of chicha and stuffed some coarse bread into his mouth. He stank of sweat and dirt and cheap hand rolled cigarettes, which he smoked continuously, but Steven was used to the smell of poor humanity.

At first he had tried to draw him out a little, to find out where he came from, about his family, but his replies were curt; it was as if he suspected Steven of trying to cross question him and resented it. Steven himself was too tired and worried to be able to spare the strength to carry on a one sided conversation.

Now they were descending from the treeless monotony of the high plateaux towards more warmth, and each twist of the road at least brought a new plant or bush to vary the texture of the hillsides and cliffs. They drove through ravines with overhanging walls draped with huge leaved plants, the rocks themselves pitted with caves.

They reached Valdavero in the evening so they could approach the Cordobes hacienda under the cover of dark, making it less likely they would be seen by the Guardia.

Steve seldom came down to the city these days and it was always possible his last visit to the hospital for supplies had been noted and recorded. Another one so soon could well arouse suspicion.

They had to cross the city. The Plaza San Marco was ringed with advertising lights and the guerilla who came from deep in the sierra was unused to town life. He almost forgot to cling to his gun as he gazed round with wonder in his dark eyes. He was really little more than a child with a veneer of toughness and sophistication, like so many of them, and underneath — naïve, unsure, ready to be led, swayed, dominated by any man who could appeal to his imagination.

In the centre of the plaza was an empty space and here couples strolled, shoeshine boys somersaulted and young children with bowls of soup waited while their mothers sold papers and sweets, and the inevitable waifs begged as they wandered like small automatons from one unknown group of grown ups to another. The hum of traffic filled the air, here and there a member of the

Guardia strolled with a gun. Steve drove a little more quickly although not fast enough to attract unwelcome attention.

Buildings, trees, electric signs passed the mud spattered windscreen. It was with great relief he saw the Cordobes' residence and swung the vehicle through the gates.

Few lights burned in the building but he hoped Don Carlos was home. The perfume of the masses of flowers filled the night air, jasmine, carnations, honeysuckle. He took a deep breath of their sweetness and then the door opened and Steve climbed down from the landrover and felt the muzzle of a gun in his back.

He was jostled up the steps and through the wide doors. One young guerilla had been left in charge of the landrover and Peggy until Steve had seen Don Carlos. He knew better than to disobey orders.

Don Carlos sat behind his carved desk, his face pale, his eyes slightly apprehensive as the young man with the gun kicked open the door without ceremony, but he gave a faint smile as he saw Steven. He wore his usual cream suit of heavy silk, a pale rose in his buttonhole. He rose to his feet and gave Steven a little bow.

As briefly as he could the latter explained the position. He was thankful Don Carlos had a quick and intelligent mind for all the information he gave him seemed to be absorbed instantly. He grasped the entire situation without so much as one small interruption. It was only by his eyes that Steven could tell the pain his story was inflicting, he guessed, too, that he must feel some bitterness towards himself, for he had known of Manuel's disappearance and what he had been involved in — but he knew, too, this was no time for explanations and recriminations.

Peggy was brought in and given some brandy and light food; a meal was prepared for Steven while arrangements were made for Keith to be contacted

. . . there was much to be done. The two young guerillas were to stay as guards on the hacienda while all was carried out to the letter. Once Don Carlos had the money from Keith and was on his way to the chapel then, and only then, Peggy could be taken to the hospital for treatment.

While they waited, Don Carlos asked Steven if he would like to go with him to see Dona Maria.

'My wife is very ill, in a coma. She will not know that I am leaving. Of course we have our own physicians, but I would like your opinion, too.'

'Of course.' With impatience now he hid his feelings, his anxiety, his longing to be on his way. Every moment that passed added to the danger to Helen, to Nicholas and Mark, but he could not refuse the old man's plea.

Dona Maria lay in the huge four poster bed, the damask curtains looped back, a small lamp standing on the table at one side with a bowl of roses and a statue of the Madonna. The blossoms filled the air with sweet perfume. In the half light it seemed almost as if the serene face of the carving looked with a calm compassion at the woman who lay, so fragile, against the silken pillows. Her eyes were closed, the lids blue veined, one hand with its long slender fingers rested on the sheet. She could have been dead instead of sleeping; it was difficult to tell unless one watched closely and saw the bed clothes rise and fall gently as she breathed. Don Carlos lifted the hand to his lips and kissed the tips of her fingers, then he turned to Steven, his cheeks wet with tears.

'She has been like this since the kidnapping. I think somehow she must have guessed about Manuel, although I do not know how. Always there was a great rapport, an empathy between them.'

Steven nodded slowly. 'Doubtless the coma is nature's way of protecting the mind. Perhaps if she could hear Manuel's voice that might recall her from the shadows, my friend.'

'There is nothing I can do here, that I realize, and I know the price if I do not obey their commands.' For a moment he looked at Steven, his eyes clouded with pain and grief. 'How our boy, our son — for that is always how I think of him, how both of us think of him — how ever he became involved with such people I do not know.'

Steven took his arm. 'Perhaps like me you are without politics, we neither oppose nor support governments, but it is not always enough to keep quiet. We have arranged our lives in other ways which we find satisfying. Perhaps today the young cannot do this, perhaps it is even our fault they cannot.'

Don Carlos patted Steven's hand. 'In the past Señor Doctor, I have maybe misunderstood you, when Manuel and Helen were young, when your wife went away, there were many things I did not understand, your attitude — I suppose I was suspicious, but I had no right to judge.' He sighed and passed his hand wearily over his brow. 'In the last hours I have learnt much, spent much time thinking. I can only say the conclusion I have come to is that I may have been wrong, selfish, blind. I thought to do no man harm was enough, but it is not. Shall we go?'

The money had been brought. Steve felt so weary he could hardly see out of his red and swollen lids. He took the heavy leather case from Keith.

For a moment the young man stood with his hand on the door of the landrover. In a low voice he said, 'Look, Doc, can't I go instead of Don Carlos? He's an old man and although he's putting on a bold front as always, the journey alone could kill him.'

'I know,' Steven said slowly, 'and bless you for suggesting it. But I fear with the mood the guerillas are in over having to release your mother they will not countenance any other alteration to their plans. It is best we fall in with them.'

'How is Helen? I feel terrible about

her because in a way if it hadn't been for the kidnap she wouldn't be involved.'

Steven put his hand on the boy's shoulder. He, too, looked near breaking point and seemed to have aged by years since the night of the party. 'You can hardly blame yourself; if anyone is at fault it is myself for being away on her first night so that she was taken to the hideout instead of me, but these things are unavoidable and we have to accept — perhaps the two saddest words in the English language are — if only . . .'

Keith glanced round; the guerilla was back in the landrover now and Don Carlos sat in the passenger seat, the bag clutched to him.

'Can't you tell me where the hideout is,' Keith said quickly, 'so I can inform da Costa?'

Steven shook his head. 'I dare not. If I did, then I am pretty certain your father, Mark, Helen, all of them would be shot out of hand immediately. This kind of game has to be played, slowly and with infinite delicacy, their way. It is like walking through a minefield. The utmost care must be taken. You will have to trust me — and Manuel . . . '

'Manuel!' Keith spat out the name as if it were gall on his tongue. 'Had it not been for him none of this business would have happened. That I do know.'

Steven turned away. There was nothing he could say in reply to this, for even in his own mind the issue was clouded, confused. All he could hope and pray was that whatever Manuel did now in some way would atone for the harm that had already occurred.

He patted Keith's shoulder.

'Go along, see to your mother, and God go with you.' Slowly he climbed into the landrover beside Don Carlos.

14

Pablo had carefully worked out the time it would take for arrangements to be made down in the city, and the journey to the chapel which was in the foothills. It would not take long from Valdavero, but from the camp it would be tedious and difficult, even dangerous. He came into the hut where Manuel was now sitting out in a chair, a blanket round his legs.

The moment had come for Nicholas to go down from the camp to the chapel — the time for the drop.

Pablo leant against the table, his arms folded, looking down at Manuel.

'So, you are better, Il Paco. Soon we shall be on the move again, out of this place.'

'Yes, once this business is over, there is still much to do, to arrange; the distribution of the food and clothes, the people will have to be told of some central point . . . '

Pablo waved aside his words with a brisk gesture of his hand. 'All that I shall arrange, I and Juanita. She has experience in these matters.'

Manuel was about to protest that he didn't realize she had ever dealt with such a situation, but Pablo swept on.

'I have decided to go myself with the gringo, Nicholas Denholm, to the drop.'

Manuel gazed at him in astonishment.

'Surely that is not necessary? You have guards you — we — can trust. It would be impossible for him, an unarmed man to escape, particularly in the terrain between here and the Chapel of the Annunciation. There is no doubt it is both a long and difficult journey.'

Pablo turned away, lighting one of the small cigars he had taken to smoking lately.

'I prefer to do it my way so long as you are here, Il Paco, and I do not trust these gringos as you do. I personally shall wish to check the money and to make sure there is no slip up. Unfortunately, as you know, it is not possible to communicate with the chapel from here; the radios we have are not powerful enough so I wish to be on the spot to see there is no slip up, no confusion or mistakes.'

He turned back to Manuel now, his eyes hidden behind the fragrant smoke of the cigar. 'You will be adequately . . . ' he paused a moment as if he had changed his mind about the end of the sentence, 'adequately looked after by the señora doctor and Flores, I am sure, also of course the boy Mark will be in your charge. He is our last hostage, to be held until all the matters are in order. That is so?'

Manuel nodded slowly. He didn't know why, but the idea of Pablo going with Nicholas had filled him with a kind of chill foreboding. He had imagined he would stay at the camp and that they would all go together eventually when the drop was completed satisfactorily. But he realized he had no alternative and there seemed little point in antagonizing Pablo who was in a slightly more expansive mood now — what difference could it make? In a way it would be more peaceful to be at the camp without his somewhat disruptive presence. But he had thought it was to be Flores who was to accompany Nicholas, that had been the original plan — Flores whom he would willingly trust with his own life. But before he had time to express his thoughts, Pablo had gone, leaving only the faint perfume of his cigar hanging on the stuffy air of the hut.

He shifted in the chair. He was impatient to be well, to be active; he hated this enforced idleness.

Nicholas heard the information that he was to have Pablo's company on the journey with dismay. He wasn't sure what he had intended to do, but he had thought there might be some way of escape from the guard — now he knew it would be hopeless. Pablo had explained the journey would be no picnic, and now he felt more edgy and nervous than ever, realizing that if he made any attempt to obtain his own freedom, he would simply endanger the lives of Peggy and Mark, to say nothing of Helen.

And so once more a vehicle left the camp, Nicholas sat between two guards in the back while Pablo was in front beside the driver.

They were all armed with rifles and revolvers and Helen watched them go with a sinking heart. Like Manuel, she somehow had a deep sense of foreboding as she saw the cloud of dust that rolled behind the disappearing jeep.

Please God, keep them all safe — keep us all safe, she prayed, looking down at Mark who clung to her once more, his childish mind completely confused by all the coming and going.

'Would you like to come and meet Manuel?' she asked at last, for the child could not be left on his own and she had to attend to the dressings, prepare some food.

She took his hand and started to walk towards the hut. As she did so she saw Flores hurrying across the compound and in through the door. She wondered what could be so urgent that it had caused him to run, something she had never seen Il Corbello do before.

Had she heard the conversation between the two men she would have been even more apprehensive for Flores had hardly got through the door before he burst out, 'Il Paco, we must get away . . . quickly. There is talk among the guerillas left on guard that Pablo intends to pick up the money for his own use.'

Manuel got to his feet, swaying as he did so.

'But there is more — worse — for it is said he intends to kill both Señor Nicholas Denholm and Don Carlos de Cordobes and at a certain hour you, the señora doctor and Mark are also to be murdered, here in the camp . . .'

15

Helen had tried to make Mark as comfortable as she could in her hut for at least she had been allowed to take him there with her. The small boy had lost weight; his eyes were like huge hollows in his little face. All Helen hoped was that he would not become seriously ill before they were finally released.

She had given him some hot soup and a hunk of the coarse bread dipped in it, but he had eaten little. He missed his mother and now, of course, his father, and Helen did the best to reassure him, but she herself felt deeply anxious about her own father — and the whole outcome of the expedition.

She managed at last to drop into a fitful sleep, her dreams filled with horror so that suddenly she woke, shivering with cold, to find a hand over her mouth. She couldn't even scream and in the darkness it was impossible to see to whom the dark form which bent over her, belonged. She was sure it must be Pablo returned either to rape or murder her. She struggled, trying to free herself but a low voice spoke now in her ear . . .

'Elena — it is I, Manuel. If I remove my hand don't make a sound. It may mean the difference between life and death if we are heard . . . '

Struggling now to sit up she breathed his name.

'Manuel — what on earth . . . ? You are shivering. Are you ill again?'

'No.' He sat now on the side of the bed. He held a small torch in one hand, its light so dim it hardly shed any beam in the darkness. She could just see that he was dressed in the inevitable uniform of camouflaged trousers and combat jacket, a peaked cap pulled down over his dark curls.

'What's the time?' She glanced at the luminous dial of her watch.

'Just after midnight. But I have a lot to tell you and not much time. Every moment that passes is precious, so please listen carefully . . . '

By now Mark was sobbing, frightened once more that something dreadful was about to happen. Helen took his hand and pulled him to her.

'Come in with me for a moment and get warm.' His small body felt thin and bitterly cold through the thin tee shirt and shorts, the only clothes he had, and which he had to wear day and night. But he snuggled into her arms and burrowed against her like a small, frightened animal, bringing tears to her eyes.

'The situation is this,' Manuel said in a voice so low she had to concentrate all her attention to hear what he said. 'Flores came to see me soon after Pablo and Nicholas had left. He told me that Pablo's intention is simply to kill the hostages.' He mentioned no names, hoping Mark would not grasp his meaning, at any rate for the moment.

Helen gasped at his words, but he put a restraining hand on her arm, holding his finger to his lips with the other hand, shaking his head slightly as he glanced at Mark. She could just see his dark eyes shining in the dim torchlight.

'He and Juanita will take the money and go, disappear . . . take it for themselves. Flores has killed two of the guerillas left to guard us. He thinks there may be more in some of the other huts, but we have no alternative now, Elena — you, the boy, Flores and myself must go as swiftly as we can after Pablo. We don't have much time for he has several hours start, but we could not attempt to leave until we are sure Flores has dealt with the total number of guerillas — it is not easy on his own. There is a short cut which I know over the mountains to the chapel. It is even more dangerous and difficult than the route Pablo had taken, but it has the advantage that only I know of it . . . it will be a terrible journey, but we have no choice.' He paused for a moment, then taking her hand in his he said, 'If you would rather not come with me, then I will go alone, but it will mean I have to leave Flores here with you as I cannot risk a woman and small boy left alone in the mountains with the possibility of bandits and roving killers everywhere . . .'

If the situation had been any other, Helen would have been forced to smile at the words, for what in reality was Manuel himself, and his rebels, but bandits? The situation was ironic; even so, she knew she had no alternative but to go with him. For one thing, in his condition it was impossible for him to drive any distance, whatever the state of the roads, and if the conditions were as bad as he said, then Flores would have to do most of the driving . . . neither did she relish being left at the camp, even with Flores as protection, and thinking of Manuel on his own, she realized that the lives of many people hung in the balance — depended on his success — Don

Carlos and her own father . . .

Even as Manuel spoke, shots rang out. He leapt to his feet, and cautiously opened the door of the hut. Flores came across the compound, his gun in his hand.

'It is the last of them, Il Paco,' he said breathlessly. 'I have flushed them from the huts. There were a half dozen altogether. Evidently Pablo had thought we would make no attempt to escape.' For a moment he leant against the door, wiping his brow.

Helen pulled on her jeans and shirt, and an old sweater of her father's he had left her. It smelt faintly of tobacco and antiseptic and for a moment it brought such a vivid picture of him before her that she felt the tears pricking behind her lids as she wondered what had happened to him, but there was no time for sentiment . . .

She lifted Mark from the little nest he had made in the blankets, and wrapped him in one of them. Flores took him from her as if he were only a little bundle of sticks, which was almost all he did seem to be.

'I put him in the jeep, Señora Doctor?'

Helen nodded, but Mark held out his arms to her.

'Please, don't leave me.' He didn't even trust the huge gentleness of Flores now.

'All right, but you'll have to wait a moment while I collect a few things together.'

Manuel had gone across to his own hut to get his gun and some ammunition, and Flores now went to the canteen, filling canvas bags and sacks with tins of soup, dried milk, chocolate and fruit — anything he could find.

As Helen stepped out into the compound with her medical bag slung over her shoulder, and Mark clinging to her hand, she saw to her horror that four of the guerillas lay sprawled in pools of their own blood where Flores had gunned them down, and she shuddered to think what would have happened by now if he had missed . . .

She hurried Mark past the bodies to the waiting jeep where Manuel was warming up the engine and loading jerricans of petrol. It was still dark as they drove out of the camp and she glanced back uneasily. She'd hated this place, and yet she had a perverse kind of affection for it because she had met Manuel again within its confines . . . perhaps the solitude of the mountains had got to her, she had heard of such things.

Manuel drove now without speaking, a preoccupied frown on his face which she could just see in the dim light. Mark snuggled down on her lap, a little easier now that they were on the move.

After about half an hour's driving, Manuel turned off the dirt road and took a narrower, rougher track over terrain that seemed even less hospitable. She glanced at him sideways, longing to ask if he really knew where he was going, but not daring to intrude on the silence.

Dawn was breaking now beyond the boulder-strewn slopes, the high snow peaks slowly etched themselves against a dark sky in lozenges of heliotrope, rose and candy pink, soon glittering pure white against an intense cobalt sky. At any other time she would have appreciated the beauty of the scene, but now she felt only sick with apprehension, with the certainty that they could never make the journey as Manuel had outlined it, and that if they did, in any case it would be too late . . .

It was perishingly cold and as if he sensed her feeling, Manuel without glancing at her, passed her a brandy flask. At first she was going to refuse, but changed her mind and took a mouthful of the raw spirit which went down her throat like living fire, bringing a momentary semblance of warmth to her limbs.

Mark seemed to sleep fitfully now, and at least the contact of his small body brought a little warmth to her own.

Although she seldom smoked, she had a crushed packet of American cigarettes in her pocket; it was an old duffle coat that Steve had given her. Now she lit two and handed one to Manuel. He took it, still without speaking, his eyes fixed on the road ahead — if it could be called that — uncertainly lit by the dim lights of the jeep, the deep cut gulleys where they travelled still shaded from the rising sun.

In a way the vast loneliness of the altiplano seemed to dwarf her fears and problems. In the distance, far below, she saw some llamas on a narrow ledge. It seemed a miracle the small amount of food the creatures could live on. She gazed out at the arid, windwhittled slopes, the high plateau with its ridges, parapets, a skyhigh world above the jungle.

The light was metallically intense now; there was a river far below, wide and straggling, threadbare scrub, cushions of ichu grass, only near the river was there cultivation.

Sometimes she dozed off, her head snapping forwards and waking her again. And just when she thought she could stand no more of the swaying, bumping, rattling movement and her cramped legs would never come back to life, suddenly Manuel drew to a stop. He turned to Flores.

'We're running low on gas, Corbello — could you fill her up from the jerrican, please.'

He got out and stood for a moment on the dirt track, stretching his arms above his head. He looked drawn, pale, years older than his age. Mark, too, had woken and was looking round him in a dazed fashion.

'It's all right, we've just stopped for a moment. We'll stretch our legs, shall we?'

He nodded and climbed down into the road, staggering a little as he did so.

Flores passed her one of the canvas bags and she found some hot coffee, some coarse bread and a few dried figs. She shared them out between the four of them.

'This isn't all we have, is it?' she queried. The huge bearded man shrugged his shoulders, glancing at Manuel for a moment.

'No, but we must be careful Señora Doctor. We do not know how long it is we have to exist on these things we have.'

She turned to Manuel. 'I didn't have time to ask you for any details back at the camp, I haven't any idea how far this journey is . . .'

He glanced away, down the bare mountain side, his eyes narrowing as he said slowly, 'The chapel from the camp, by the route Pablo took, is about four days' journey, they have a few hours start, but the way we are going, it should only take us two days and two nights.' He hesitated and Helen broke in.

'You don't mean that we have to travel day and night with no rest?'

He nodded. 'That is what we should do.'

She scrambled to her feet from where she had sat down on a rock.

'But that's madness! In your state you'll make yourself seriously ill. You shouldn't be driving at all.'

'I know that, but other people's lives are at stake, many people's. It is a question of priorities,' he sighed wearily, 'but I will tell Flores the route for the rest of the day. Till dark at least he can drive. I sit beside him and you in the back with the little one.'

It was an order, not a request, and she and Mark climbed into the back. Manuel covered them with the sacks and old blankets they had brought.

'If we make good time, then perhaps tonight we can rest for a little. It is difficult anyway to find the track in the dark.'

Thank goodness for that, she thought, spending the next few hours almost as if in some kind of delirium; at times it seemed impossible the jeep could negotiate the track. They hung above enormous canyons whose base she could not see, and she closed her eyes, clenching her fists, expecting any moment they would be thrown over the cliff as the loose edge of the road gave way, and that they would roll over and over hundreds of feet to the river below. They slid down inclines that seemed perpendicular, and then climbed what appeared to be the side of a building to a flat plain surrounded by thick white clouds with patches of blue sky . . . then at last they were running down hill again.

'This is an old Inca highway,' Manuel said. 'It is not on any map, but I know it from the past. Many of these exist, unchartered, if one is lucky they continue in the direction one needs to take.' But almost as he uttered the words, the track ended and became a mass of boulders. For a moment they sat in silence as Flores switched off the engine. Then suddenly he exclaimed.

'Look, Señor, it is a shepherd's hut, I think.'

Helen looked in the direction he was pointing, and there was a primitive, windowless hovel huddled as if for shelter, under a boulder which stuck out from the side of the mountain. The walls were made of granite boulders with a rough thatch roof, but the thought of being able to lie down, even on the floor, in a sleeping bag and stretch her cramped limbs seemed like a glimpse of paradise to Helen.

They all got out of the jeep, Flores unslung his gun.

'Sometimes it can be an Indian who is not friendly,' he said softly. 'Wait here, Il Paco, and I will see.'

Manuel nodded. 'I'll keep you covered, Flores.'

Even as he spoke the door was opened and an old man stood in the dusk. Flores lowered his gun and stepped forwards. He exchanged a few words with him and then came back to where they waited.

'It is well, he is a shepherd, but he lives in the hut all the time. His own home was burned down by marauding rebels some time ago and the village sacked. There is not much room but he will gladly give us shelter for the night.'

Mark seemed a little more lively now and was interested and fascinated by the old man and his rather mangy dog. Helen longed to tell him not to touch it but dared not for fear of offending the old man.

Inside the air was foetid for there was no window and all the light came from two tallow candles stuck to the wall with strips of sticking plaster. There was a crude bamboo bed supported on stakes, a stone shelf covered with sheepskin. Corn cobs and drying skins hung from the rafters and earthenware cooking pots stood round the fire. The old man was drawing on a ragged coat and explaining to Manuel that he had to go out and round up some sheep and llamas which had strayed to the other side of the mountain but they were welcome to make use of his humble home.

'We have some food with us,' Manuel said, 'which we shall be glad to share but we have to be frugal for we have a long journey still ahead.' The old man nodded, content to have no further explanation for their sudden appearance. Manuel turned to Flores.

'If our friend does not object, go with him, amigo. He will perhaps be able to show you the track, and on the way back you can fill the water bottles from the stream.' Flores nodded and followed the old man out of the hut. Manuel produced some bitter chocolate which he heated in one of the pots over the fire, and there was toasted maize which he called cancha. Much to Helen's relief Mark ate with a certain amount of appetite, but Manuel picked at his food, studying a map he had brought from his pocket, and lighting one cigarette from another.

Helen got up at last. 'Let me look at your dressing. It should be changed. I have a fresh one with me.'

He shook his head impatiently. 'No, it

213

is not necessary. Best leave it as it is.'

She felt too weary to insist. She packed what was left of the food back in the bag and then put Mark on the small bed and covered him over. Almost immediately he fell asleep, his long lashes making dark lines on his pale cheeks. She stood for a moment looking down at him and did not hear Manuel come up behind until she felt his hands on her shoulders and gently he turned her round to face him. In the dim light of the candles he looked a little more relaxed now he had eaten. Just for a moment it was like they had once been — the boy and the girl — now she wondered if that love she had felt had been just the extension of their childhood closeness. They had loved one another deeply and sincerely, in fact she had been sure she would never love again . . . now she felt all mixed up; she was no longer sure that what they had once shared was the only kind of love — or what it was she had felt briefly, but intensely, for Keith . . .

As if he were reading her thoughts, he said, 'I have heard talk from Steve of this Keith — the son of Nicholas. You came on the boat with him . . . '

She nodded. He had caught her unawares. She had no idea Steve had talked to Manuel of him.

'He was a friend, yes — a shipboard acquaintance.'

Somehow she felt disloyal, and knew she sounded unconvincing and that he didn't believe her. Aware of this she tried to loosen his hold on her. His dark eyes were gently mocking but warm at least and with an amused smile on his lips he said slowly, 'I was beginning to think, seeing how efficient you are, that that was all there was to you now, Elena. One of the very self-sufficient women, all efficiency and no passion.'

The colour rushed to her cheeks now as he drew her into his arms, and before she could resist, tilted up her chin and kissed her full on the mouth.

She didn't want to resist. Her mind produced instant protests which never reached her lips. This was really what she had come half across the world for, this was what she wanted, dreamed about . . . the feel of his strength, the hardness of his body against hers.

She returned his kiss and his became longer, harder as she slipped her arms round his neck.

She closed her eyes and forgot their surroundings, their problems, their terrible anxieties, she felt his heart beat against hers in answering rhythm.

For a moment she opened her eyes to see the wonder and desire in his.

She closed them again and stopped wondering about anything . . .

16

They left before dawn had broken the next morning. Flores had drawn a rough map of the route the shepherd had shown him, taking them back on to some kind of track, although it was still terribly rough. He drove now and Manuel and Helen sat in the back of the truck with Mark between them. Manuel had started to bleed again in spite of all the skill with which Helen had tried to staunch the blood, some of the stitches had become infected because of lack of drugs and she knew it was absolutely imperative that he be got to hospital.

'Can't we get on to a proper road and go down to Valdavero?' she said at last, watching his pale, taut face, feeling with him the terrible jolts and bumps the vehicle made over the terrain, each one of which must have been like a knife thrust into his wound. But although he had bitten his lip until the blood ran, he shook his head.

'No, Elena. We have to reach the chapel before Pablo — don't you see — I have to save Don Carlos, I have to.' He struck the palm of one hand with the fist of the other, his eyes blazing as he thought of the treachery of Pablo. Helen knew it was all he could think about now and she realized it had become a complete obsession as he felt in some way it would atone for all he had done to Don Carlos and Maria.

She knew it was no good to argue with him; all she could do was to try to give him the best medical attention she could under the circumstances, and try and keep his mind off Pablo, a task she knew was more or less impossible, but at least it was worth the effort. Also it was the first chance she had had to talk to him about his future, his intentions, and even his past for the conversations they had managed to have had been intermittent.

'How do people round here make a living?' she said now slowly. She looked at the barren landscape with mounting dismay and horror. Mark was asleep in her arms, his face still pale although he had managed to eat some of the food the old shepherd had provided for breakfast, quite enjoying the yuca root which had been baking in the embers all night, and then been split open by the shepherd to show the soft inside, like a baked potato, and smeared with some sour llama milk. It hadn't been particularly appetizing, but Mark had seemed hungry. He was the only member of the party who was quite enjoying the hazardous, uncomfortable trip, and had even taken an interest in the surrounding countryside which he said reminded him of the westerns on the telly.

Manuel hesitated, turning her question over in his mind, then, taking her hand in his, he said slowly, 'I suppose you thought you were coming to a peaceful country, Elena, that this ancient land is without trouble, but it is not so. Many of the peasants have arms, many fear another revolution like that of nineteen fifty-two. All this stirred up by agitators.' He paused a moment, then went on, 'I fear now that Pablo is one of them. That all the time I had believed in him this was really his motive.'

'You mean he's a communist?'

'Yes, the money he hopes to get from Don Carlos will, I am sure, be spent on arms and ammunition . . . that is partly why we must get to the chapel first.' He looked away from her. 'I have never had time for politics, never been involved in them, but the agitators won't listen, people like Pablo, and in some ways they don't realize the Indian has fooled the communist — but this, too, can only lead to bloodshed.'

She didn't altogether understand what he meant. The day seemed endless — they drove through gorges, across mountainsides, along zig zag tracks which were little more than mule trails, around the tips of precipices, stopping only for a bite of food, a drink of the coffee they had made at the hut, and to refill the tank with petrol which was running dangerously low for the terrain itself was a source of using more fuel than would have been a flat road. At one time it seemed to her they had left civilization behind forever in the rain and windswept cactus-studded high pastureland. They had even seen a pack of Andean sheepdogs who had evidently turned rogue and hunted almost like wolves ... and then when she thought she could take no more, they started to drop down into softer landscape, following runs made by bear, wild pig and puma, Manuel told her. Occasionally Flores had to get out of the jeep to chop through thorn and bamboo which had overgrown the track, with his machete. Each time they made a brief stop for this, Helen had the feeling the forest around them must have been alive with game but she was conscious most strongly of the dark green silence beneath interlaced branches, a moist and absolute stillness broken only occasionally by stealthy drippings from the damp patches of foliage . . . a sheer weight of silence, choking oppression under a blanket of sweat, dust, steam and insects in complete contrast to the bitter cold they had felt higher up.

And then at last, as dusk started to fall, Manuel touched Flores' shoulder.

'Stop here amigo.'

Painfully, slowly, he got down from the jeep telling Helen and Mark to stay where they were. Ahead in a clearing stood what had once been a small Indian village composed of adobe huts, now derelict, their roofs fallen in, the walls crumbling. A thin dog scratched among the scraps, beyond there was no sign of life . . . but there was a larger thatched building surrounded by a crude rectangular wall with a stone-roofed gateway. It had a small baked mud tower with a white cross on the top — the chapel. She knew they were to be found scattered all over the area. Where they found enough folk to make up a congregation, she didn't know, but obviously this one had been abandoned long ago. As far as she could see there was no sign that Pablo and Nicholas had arrived — nor Don Carlos and Steven. At least that meant a short respite — she wasn't sure if she was glad or sorry, for it would mean a tense waiting time and that was perhaps going to be the hardest part of all.

Manuel came back, almost doubled up now with the pain of his wound, ashen faced with the loss of blood. Helen got down from the jeep and went to meet him, putting her arms round him to give him some support. She was angry — furious — not with him, but with the system, the madness that had led to this . . .

'*You must go to hospital.*' She emphasized each word as if she were trying to get the message through to a child — or an idiot. 'Don't you see, you'll die if you don't.'

He looked at her, his eyes still burning with an inner fire like dark coals.

'If I were to go now I would rather be dead. I have a debt to pay, a debt I have owed for many years — I may not be a man of honour — anyway in your eyes, Elena, and perhaps you are right, but I still have some pride left. Dona Maria has been much in my thoughts these last few hours; it is as if she speaks with me, I can see her so clearly, she is depending on me to protect Don Carlos — this to me now is all that matters.' He paused a moment and somehow from his pain wracked body a smile welled up — a lop sided grin. 'At least, almost all, I think you know what else is of importance.' He bent and kissed her gently on the lips without passion, but with a tenderness so great that tears sprung to her eyes. Then he said, 'Come, we must hide the jeep and do the best we can to conceal ourselves in the chapel. We do not know who will arrive first. If it is Don Carlos and Steve then we have a chance to hide them, to protect them — if it is otherwise — I do not know but at least we shall be a surprise.'

Flores parked the jeep behind the chapel in the thick, lush undergrowth which had invaded the building. Creepers twined round the broken walls, the roof hung in tatters and little pools of water had formed among the broken tiles of the floor. But at least there was some kind of shelter and protection. It was getting dark and cold and they huddled together for they did not dare to make a fire.

Now and then there was the sound of rustling in the surrounding trees. Fear clutched at Helen's heart and throat like something tangible; fear was a hot, dry taste in her mouth. She felt as if she would be smothered beneath the blanket of humidity. Then she started to shiver. She wasn't sure if it was the same fear or the chill from the dampness that seemed to descend all around them now from the forest with the rising of the moon . . . and then suddenly there was the rumble of distant thunder, wind stirred through the forest, lashing the crowns of the trees into a frenzy, and the rain fell in a solid sheet as they cringed beneath a piece of masonry in the primitive wall that gave a little shelter — and then, when she thought she could stand it no longer, the sound of the rain on the rotting reed of the roof and the huge leaves of the trees — the storm ceased and steam rose from all around as if from a hundred boiling kettles. A great stillness, a silence that seemed to throb with menace after the tumult of the storm.

Then, almost as if it were a part of the noise of the jungle, on the still air came the sound of an engine . . . a vehicle engine . . . coming closer.

Flores got to his feet, his rifle at the ready, Helen heard the click as he cocked it . . . Manuel, too, struggled up, having to push himself against the crumbling stones, and a feeling of utter helplessness swept over Helen as she watched him. Her arms were tightly round Mark who had hidden his head on her breast when the storm broke, and was crying silently like a small wounded animal, a sound far worse than if he had sobbed out loud . . . but Manuel had so impressed upon them the need for absolute quiet that he had automatically obeyed the order to the letter and scarcely dared to breathe.

Now the two men stood silhouetted against the moonlight which filled the clearing once more. From far away, twin lights pierced the night sky, wavering, changing course, somehow holding a deep sense of foreboding, a growing menace. Helen felt as if the blood in her veins had literally turned to ice. None of them knew if it would be Don Carlos and Steve or Pablo, and so much depended on the outcome.

At last the vehicle was almost on them and it ground to a halt. There was the clatter of rifles, men's voices — and a woman's speaking rapidly in Spanish

. . . Helen let out her breath on a long sigh. It was Pablo with Nicholas and Juanita . . . but how far behind were Don Carlos and Steve? Obviously now as they intended to kill them there would be an ambush . . . would they first shoot Nicholas or let him collect the money so that everything appeared normal, and then shoot. She clenched her hands until the nails cut into the palms and she felt the warm blood flow.

Flores moved slightly and the moonlight caught the barrel of his rifle . . .

She held her breath, waiting for the fusilade of shots she was sure must be imminent, but Pablo and Juanita were still talking in low voices as if they feared they would be overheard . . . by whom? Helen wondered.

Manuel crouched down again and whispered against her ear, 'Keep right down on the ground and don't let the boy make a sound or move . . . we have to wait till they approach the chapel and it's possible they may not, at least until they hear Don Carlos and your father coming. Whatever happens remember our lives depend on absolute silence.'

She breathed her assent, he got slowly to his feet again . . . footsteps were coming towards the chapel. She felt rather than saw Flores tense his muscles.

'What is the point of coming in here?' Nicholas said. 'Surely if they are to arrive at any moment we might as well wait in the jeep. That place looks dangerous in the extreme.' There was the sound of a fist meeting flesh and a scream of pain . . . Helen felt Mark move instinctively and she held him even more tightly, her lips now against his ear as she whispered to him.

'Quiet, love. Whatever happens they mustn't know we are here.'

A man stood in the half ruined doorway of the chapel, bareheaded — Helen recognized Nicholas' outline and prayed he wouldn't see them in the corner where they crouched. Just as he stumbled forward she saw Pablo, too, his rifle unslung as he pushed Nicholas forward with the butt.

'Wait there, gringo, till I tell you — '
He broke off as the sound of another
engine came with the breeze. Once
more lights raked the darkness and
once more Helen felt the bitter taste of
fear in her mouth.

Pablo shouted something to the
guerillas who waited by the jeep and
she heard their rifles clatter as they got
into position. She longed to call out, to
shout to Steve and tell him the terrible
danger he was approaching ... why
didn't Manuel or Flores shoot at Pablo
now? Then she realized Nicholas was
standing in direct line of fire ... if only
he would move ...

And then everything happened at
once and all hell was let loose. A shot
rang out. Who fired it she had no idea,
but suddenly the small compound
outside the chapel seemed to be alive
with men, with flashes of gunfire and
smoke, shouts, curses ... Nicholas had
disappeared as had Manuel and Flores
... she longed to get up and go to the

door, to see for herself what had happened, but she knew she must obey Manuel's orders. She held Mark tightly to her, and now the child spoke, calling to Nicholas.

'Daddy! We're here. Please come, please help us.' Out of the shadows Nicholas moved towards them, his face pouring with blood from where he had been shot.

'Mark! Helen! Good God, how on earth . . . ' Before he could say more or they reply, more shots were fired and there was the sound of two or three more vehicles arriving with no lights. All was confusion as Helen thrust Mark now into Nicholas' arms and tripping over loose stones and pieces of timber, ran forwards to the doorway. The sight that met her eyes was like a battlefield . . . a man crouched down behind the nearest vehicle and she could see it was Manuel, a jeep the other side had caught fire and the flames lit up the whole scene like something from a nightmare.

She murmured his name, but either he didn't hear or was in too vulnerable a position to move. As she spoke, a head appeared on the other side of the vehicle, and then the shoulders and a rifle held in the firing position. She saw it was Pablo and he was aiming at the jeep where Steve and Don Carlos still sat, behind them a police Range Rover, their headlights full on. She couldn't see inside them but two policemen and a guerilla lay on the ground, either mortally wounded or dead, she could not tell.

As she watched, slowly, painfully, Manuel got to his feet and with a swiftness she had not thought possible in his terribly weak condition, he fired . . .

Pablo spun round, for a moment his eyes gleamed in the moonlight, then he slumped out of sight behind the vehicle. She was about to step forward when she felt something sting her ear making a noise like an angry wasp, while at the same moment there was a flash and

Manuel fell to the ground. Nicholas shouted to her to get down but as if she had no will power of her own, she went on, throwing herself down beside Manuel. Blood was pumping from a wound in his chest, already his eyes were glazing as saliva and blood ran from his mouth . . .

'Manuel . . . Manuel . . . please don't die . . . please . . . ' The words came out on a long shuddering sob and even as she uttered them she knew it was hopeless. She lifted his head on to her lap, bending down as he tried to move his lips, for a moment his eyelids fluttered.

'Elena . . . amigo . . . my love . . . '

She kissed the pale dirty cheek as his whole body sagged, his head rolling to one side. For a moment she forgot where she was, forgot everything that had happened, she was a girl again and Manuel her lover as she screamed his name. He didn't move, his eyes open now, sightless in the moonlight . . .

She was scarcely conscious of what

was going on around her but she felt someone take her arm, drawing her gently to her feet.

'It's no use, honey,' a voice said softly. 'He's dead. Here, drink this.' A brandy flask was held to her lips. For a moment she turned her head away, then as if she had changed her mind, she drank deeply and the liquid ran like fire along her veins . . .

'Keith! How on earth . . . ?'

'Never mind about that. Come on, honey. We must get you and Dad back to hospital as quickly as we can.'

She looked round. 'Mark . . . '

'He's O.K.'

'I can't leave . . . him . . . ' She turned and looked down at Manuel where he lay in an ever widening pool of scarlet.

'You have to,' he said gently. 'Don't worry. I'll make sure he's taken care of.'

She saw her father now, leaning against the door of the jeep. Don Carlos still sat in the passenger seat, the bag of money on his knee. For a moment she thought bitterly that that was the cause of all the misery, the deaths, the waste of life. The old man's usually immaculate suit was creased and dirty, his hair dishevelled, but still he looked what he was — a true aristocrat, dignified, proud . . . he caught sight of Helen.

'My child, you are hurt.'

She stumbled towards him, Keith's arm round her.

'It's nothing, only a graze, but how are you?'

He looked at her, his eyes dark as the forest about them, but he said with a lift of his head, 'He saved my life — Manuel Ortega Cordobes saved his father's life.'

Mark was held fast in his father's arms and now Keith drew her to him and kissed her fully on the lips.

'I know this is hardly the time or the place — but I love you.'

For a moment she stood, uncertain . . .

'Where do I go from here?' she murmured to herself.

'It's a helluva long way from S.A. to London . . . '

She nodded. 'I know, but there's a longer journey that I have to make, and I'm not sure of the ending . . . I'm not sure even how the story itself ends . . . '

He grinned, the dear, familiar grin she remembered from that other world on board ship that seemed a lifetime away. He helped her into the back of the police Range Rover and climbed in beside her.

'I can wait till you solve the problem, honey. I've learned to be very good at waiting the last few weeks; something I've never done before.'

As he spoke, the sky suddenly lightened as the sun came from behind the mountains.

'Another day,' he sighed. His eyes were on the ridges, snow covered, that towered away above them. ' 'Night's candles are burnt out.' I can't quite remember how Will ended that quote.'

Helen smiled at him for a moment. ' 'and jocund day stands tiptoe on the misty mountain tops.''

She turned and looked once more at Manuel where he lay, his face somehow serene, younger — as she remembered it. The tears sprang behind her lids and she let them fall unchecked. 'It's such a waste, so much youth, so much energy, so much love — so much to live for, all wasted.'

Keith took her face in his hands and turned it slowly towards him so that she was looking straight into his eyes.

'Not altogether. He saved the life of the man he loved, perhaps more than anyone, the man who had given him life itself. Perhaps that is a measure of success, of a life worth the living, a death worth the giving . . . who can say?'

She let her head fall on his shoulder as she said softly, suddenly so weary, so drained that she could make no more effort, 'Just take me home, please.'

'Of course — for 'when the journey's over there'll be time enough for sleep . . .''

We do hope that you have enjoyed reading this large print book.

Did you know that all of our titles are available for purchase?

We publish a wide range of high quality large print books including:
Romances, Mysteries, Classics
General Fiction
Non Fiction and Westerns

Special interest titles available in large print are:
The Little Oxford Dictionary
Music Book, Song Book
Hymn Book, Service Book

Also available from us courtesy of Oxford University Press:
Young Readers' Dictionary
(large print edition)
Young Readers' Thesaurus
(large print edition)

For further information or a free brochure, please contact us at:
Ulverscroft Large Print Books Ltd.,
The Green, Bradgate Road, Anstey,
Leicester, LE7 7FU, England.
Tel: (00 44) 0116 236 4325
Fax: (00 44) 0116 234 0205

Other titles in the
Linford Romance Library:

DANGER COMES CALLING

Karen Abbott

Elaine Driscoe and her sister Kate expect their walking holiday along Offa's Dyke Path to be a peaceful pursuit — until a chance encounter with a mysterious stranger casts a shadow of fear over everything. Their steps are constantly crossed by three men — Niall, Steve and Phil. But which of them can they trust? And what is the ultimate danger that awaits them in Prestatyn?

NO SUBSTITUTE FOR LOVE

Dina McCall

Although recently made redundant, nurse Holly Fraser decides to spend some of her savings on a Christmas coach tour in Scotland. When the tour reaches the Callender Hotel, several people mistake Holly for a Mrs MacEwan. Furthermore, Ian MacEwan arrives to take her to the Hall, convinced that she is his wife, Carol! Although Ian despises Carol for having deserted him and their two small children, two-year-old Lucy needs her mother. Holly stays to help the child, but finds herself in an impossible situation.

LOVE'S SWEET SECRETS

Bridget Thorn

When her parents die, Melanie comes home to run their guest house and to try to win the Jubilee Prize for her father's garden. But her sister, Angela, wants her to sell the property, and her boyfriend, Michael, wants a partnership and marriage. Just before the Spring opening, Paul Hunt arrives and helps Melanie when the garden is attacked by vandals. After the news is splashed over the national papers, guests cancel. Then real danger threatens. But who is the enemy?

OUT OF THE SHADOWS

Judy Chard

Why does Carol Marsh, the new receptionist at the country inn in Devon, have to report to the police regularly? Why does she never ask for time off and rejects all attempts by the owner, Norman Willis, to be friendly? Then, Norman's wife is found dead in suspicious circum-stances. Could Carol have had some part in her death? Yvonne's relationship with her husband had deteriorated since Carol's arrival. Maybe Carol and Norman have a deeper, more sinister relationship than that of employer and employee.